PRAISE FC
KATIE MacALISTER

Memoirs of a Dragon Hunter

"Bursting with the author's trademark zany humor and spicy romance . . . this quick tale will delight paranormal romance fans."—*Publishers Weekly*

Sparks Fly

"Balanced by a well-organized plot and MacAlister's trademark humor."—*Publishers Weekly*

It's All Greek to Me

"A fun and sexy read."—The Season for Romance

"A wonderful lighthearted romantic romp as a kick-butt American Amazon and a hunky Greek find love. Filled with humor, fans will laugh with the zaniness of Harry meets Yacky."—*Midwest Book Review*

Much Ado About Vampires

"A humorous take on the dark and demonic."—*USA Today*

"Once again this author has done a wonderful job. I was sucked into the world of Dark Ones right from the start and was taken on a fantastic ride. This book is full of witty dialogue and great romance, making it one that should not be missed."—Fresh Fiction

The Unbearable Lightness of Dragons

"Had me laughing out loud. . . . This book is full of humor and romance, keeping the reader entertained all the way through . . . a wondrous story full of magic. . . . I cannot wait to see what happens next in the lives of the dragons."—Fresh Fiction

Also By Katie MacAlister

Dark Ones Series
A Girl's Guide to Vampires
Sex and the Single Vampire
Sex, Lies, and Vampires
Even Vampires Get the Blues
Bring Out Your Dead (Novella)
The Last of the Red-Hot Vampires
Crouching Vampire, Hidden Fang
Unleashed (Novella)
In the Company of Vampires
Confessions of a Vampire's Girlfriend
Much Ado About Vampires
A Tale of Two Vampires
The Undead in My Bed (Novella)
The Vampire Always Rises

Dragon Sept Series
You Slay Me
Fire Me Up
Light My Fire
Holy Smokes
Death's Excellent Vacation (short story)
Playing WIth Fire
Up In Smoke
Me and My Shadow
Love in the Time of Dragons
The Unbearable Lightness of Dragons
Sparks Fly
Dragon Fall
Dragon Storm
Dragon Soul
Dragon Unbound
Dragonblight

Dragon Hunter Series
Memoirs of a Dragon Huner
Day of the Dragon

Born Prophecy Series
Fireborn
Starborn
Shadowborn

Time Thief Series
Time Thief
Time Crossed (short story)
The Art of Stealing Time

Matchmaker in Wonderland Series
The Importance of Being Alice
A Midsummer Night's Romp
Daring in a Blue Dress
Perils of Paulie

Papaioannou Series
It's All Greek to Me
Ever Fallen in Love
A Tale of Two Cousins

Contemporary Single Titles
Improper English
Bird of Paradise (Novella)
Men in Kilts
The Corset Diaries
A Hard Day's Knight
Blow Me Down
You Auto-Complete Me

Noble Historical Series
Noble Intentions
Noble Destiny
The Trouble With Harry
The Truth About Leo

Paranormal Single Titles
Ain't Myth-Behaving

Mysteries
Ghost of a Chance

Steampunk Romance
Steamed

To Jess A with many warm fuzzies, and lots of appreciation for all your support!

WHAT EXACTLY IS THIS?

Since I know there are probably more than a few of you who are even now squinting at this book and muttering to yourself, "Where does this fit in with the other dragon books?" I thought a quick explanation and clarification would be timely.

Here's the explanation part: In January 2020 (remember the time before the pandemic?), I had the brilliant idea of publishing a story that covered the time period between the end of *Sparks Fly* (aka the third Light Dragons book) and the beginning of *Dragon Fall.*

Why would I do that? Mostly because I'd switched publishers at that point, and since the new dragon publisher wanted the three Dragon Fall books (*Dragon Fall, Dragon Storm*, and *Dragon Soul*) to be different from the other sept books, I decided to break the weyr apart, and let those three books tell how it was re-formed.

In my head, it worked wonderfully. I dribbled out just enough information in *Dragon Fall* that readers would instantly be caught up, and be ready to move forward with seeing how the dragonkin fixed everything. Reality … well, reality was a lot different from what went on in my head.

It so often is.

In truth, readers were confused, with lots and lots and lots of people writing to ask me for the name of the book that covered how the dragons were cursed, etc. It quickly became apparent that what made perfect sense in my mind did not make perfect sense to a whole lot of readers.

Which brings me back to January 2020. I figured I'd finally write a novella that covered all the happenings that went down in my head while I was writing the Dragon Fall books. I released one episode each month to newsletter subscribers only, and allowed myself to play with the story, writing each chapter from a different point of view. That let me bring back Aisling and Drake, May and Gabriel, and even Jim as a narrator (amongst others).

Once the serialized version was finished, I sat down to edit the book, and realized there were still a lot of things I had yet to explain, and I more than doubled the length of the original serialized version that newsletter readers saw. Hopefully, I covered all the remaining questions.

If you are current on the dragon books through *Dragon Soul* (or *Dragon Unbound*, which follows it), then *Dragonblight* will explain just how things came about before those last few books. If you are new to the books, then slot this one just after *Sparks Fly*, and before *Dragon Fall*.

Since I don't want anyone more confused than they might be by the appearance of an "in-between" book, here's a list of the reading order of all the dragon books, with the main protagonists and important secondary characters.

Aisling Grey Novels

· YOU SLAY ME
· FIRE ME UP
· LIGHT MY FIRE
· HOLY SMOKES
· "Perils of Effrijim" novella (originally in DEATH'S EXCELLENT VACATION anthology)

Main Characters:
Aisling Grey, Guardian
Drake Vireo, wyvern of the green dragons
Effrijim (aka Jim), demon in Newfoundland dog form

Silver Dragon Novels

· PLAYING WITH FIRE
· UP IN SMOKE
· ME AND MY SHADOW

Main Characters:
May Northcott, doppelganger
Gabriel Tauhou, wyvern of the silver dragons
Cyrene Northcott, May's twin, a naiad
Magoth, demon lord to whom Cyrene bound May upon her creation
Kawaa, Gabriel's shaman mother
Sally, ex–demon lord and, with her work partner Terrin

Light Dragon Novels

· LOVE IN THE TIME OF DRAGONS
· THE UNBEARABLE LIGHTNESS OF DRAGONS
· SPARKS FLY

Main Characters:
Ysolde de Bouchier
Baltic, former wyvern of the black dragons, and current wyvern of the light dragons

Brom, Ysolde's son with her ex-husband, Gareth

Pavel, Baltic's best friend and right-hand man

Holland, Pavel's romantic partner

Thala, daughter of a famed archimage, who stole a valuable sword owned by Baltic

Katie Explains to Readers What Happened After-the-Fact Novel

DRAGONBLIGHT

Dragon Fall Novels

DRAGON FALL

Main characters:

Aoife Ndala Dakar, sister of Bee and Rowan

Kostya (Konstantin) Fekete, brother to Drake, and wyvern of the black dragons

DRAGON STORM

Main characters:

Bee Dakar, sister of Rowan and Aoife

Constantine of Norka, godfather of Kostya, and former wyvern of the silver dragons

Gary (aka Gareth), a disembodied head whom Constantine and Bee adopt

DRAGON SOUL

Main characters:

Sophea Long, widow of Jian Tin (wyvern of the red dragons)

Rowan Dakar, brother of Aoife and Bee, and later wyvern of the red dragons

Mrs. Papadopoulos, mysterious old lady

DRAGON UNBOUND

Main characters:

Charity, siren

The First Dragon, demigod who created all dragons who ever were, and who ever will be

Dragon Hunter Novels

MEMOIRS OF A DRAGON HUNTER

Main characters:

Veronica James, math teacher

Ian Iskandar, dragon hunter

Sasha, Ian's apprentice

DAY OF THE DRAGON

Main characters:

Thaisa Moore, medieval scholar

Archer Andras, master of the storm dragons, and twin of Hunter Vehar

Hunter Vehar, master of the shadow dragons

Bree, Sasha's sister

My dear Friia,

I take pen in hand—or, in this case, keyboard under fingers—to respond to your electronic letter that my steward informed me you sent to me last week. I am sure there must be a reason you chose to converse in this medium rather than simply visiting me, as you have been wont to do over the centuries, but regardless, your missive was most interesting. I am pleased to know that you are enjoying your time with the dolphins in the Caribbean, although I had thought Asgard was bound to one of the Norse lands. When did you move it?

You ask about my kin. I wish I might give as good an account as you have of your people, but there has been a disturbance gathering in the life force of all dragonkin. After much thought as to how best to aid my children, I have begun to set it into motion.

My regards to Óðinn.

Your devoted brother,
First Dragon

ONE

IN WHICH AISLING SEDUCES A DRAGON

"There are imps, imps everywhere. Hundreds of them. No, thousands. One can't step foot without almost squashing one into the pavement. Is that not right, Javier?"

Javier, his cheeks bulging with items from the plate of appetizers that he was sharing with the woman on my right, nodded and gave a few frantic chews before gulping down his mouthful of spring roll and sashimi. "Most definitely. Far too many imp squashings. It is not good for the shoes, you know?"

"And what must the tourists think?" continued my neighbor, scrunching up her nose in a way that looked both adorable and whimsical.

I wondered if I could pull off such a thing, and glanced down the long length of the bar. There was no one upon whom I could practice my nose-scrunching. I sighed, and took another pull on the frosted lemonade. "The tourists?" I asked the woman, trying to distract myself.

"The mundane ones, you know?" She gave a very Gallic tch in the back of her throat, her accent some variation on French that was unfamiliar to me. She had almost a singsong lilt that had me eyeing her with curiosity. "The pipples who are not in the Otherworld."

"Ah, yes, those pipples." I nodded, and pushed my now-empty glass away.

"It cannot be good for the tourist pipples to see imp guts everywhere. Questions must be asked at the sight of squashed imps. Questions that are most hard to answer. What are you going to do?"

"Me?" I stopped myself in the middle of checking my phone for any messages. I'd made a mental promise earlier that I wouldn't fuss, and I'd be damned if I gave in after only three hours. "I didn't know I was supposed to clean up imp remains."

"But you are a Guardian," the woman replied, swiveling on the barstool to give me a pointed look. "It is your job to protect everyone from imps, yes? That includes the mundane tourists."

"There are two Guardians who manage the Paris portals, imps included," I told her, signaling to the bartender for another iced lemonade. "It would be rude of me to push my way in and take over their job, not to mention highly impractical. I won't be in Paris long enough to do more than swab up a few smeared remains. Yes, please, another one. It's very hot out for June, and I got a bit overheated shopping in the market."

"Bah," the woman said, snapping off the end of a deep-fried pickle. "It is your job to protect us. The others who you say guard the portals, they do nothing."

"It is problematic," her friend Javier agreed, chewing quickly to get rid of his mouthful of toasted ravioli. I gave the ravioli a long look, wondering if a little snack wasn't in order after my morning spent combing the antique shops and open-air stalls for the perfect birthday present. "But, Carmina, it is not this lady's problem, our imp situation. We must speak to Jovana."

"Bah," she repeated, and gave a sniff that spoke volumes. "She has no interest in anything but some mage sword. You are new to Paris, Guardian?"

"Not really, no, I just haven't been here much since my children were born," I said, smiling and tucking my phone away lest I make stabby taps on the face of a certain annoying dragon. "That was about two and a half years ago."

"Much has changed in that time," the woman, evidently named Carmina, said with a dark look at her companion.

He nodded again. "Things are happening. There are currents beneath, you understand?"

"Deep currents," Carmina said with another snap at her fried pickle. "But come, we are being most annoying, are we not? We have done nothing but talk about us, and not discussed in what way we can help you enjoy Paris."

I blinked a couple of times—bad habit, that—while I wondered when I'd asked for help. I'd entered into friendly conversation with the couple when I sat down at the bar, but I didn't realize they thought I was seeking advice by doing so. "I appreciate the offer, but I don't really need help. Not in that way. I'm a bit ..." I made a vague gesture, then giggled. "Sorry, it's just that I've got an itch that hasn't been scratched in a long time."

"An itch?" Javier glanced down at my sundress with accompanying bare arms. "You have a rash of some sort?"

"Javier, do not embarrass me with your so very manness in front of this Guardian." Carmina cast him a look filled with gentle chiding before leaning in close to his ear, and adding in a clearly audible whisper, "It is sex that is the itch. She is seeking the engagement most sexual."

"Ah," he said, his gaze flitting over me again, this time in an impersonal assessment. I sat up a little straighter, wishing I'd done something with my hair, which, as ever, was living its own life without regards as to how I desired it to behave. "That is so, yes, I see. Itch that hasn't been scratched. You permit?"

He had pulled out a small navy blue notebook and a tiny mechanical pencil, holding it poised over the paper.

"Javier collects interesting phrases in the English," Carmina explained.

"Does he? By all means, then, collect away."

"Now." Carmina folded her hands and gave me her full attention. "You will tell us what you are looking for in a partner sexual, and we will help you find this scratcher of the itch. Is it a male or female you seek, or do you have a preference? Corporeal or not? Are beings of the nature most dark enticing to your itch, or do you prefer less intense relationships?"

I opened my mouth to tell her that I wasn't looking for anyone since I had a perfectly good itch-scratcher of my own, but at that moment, the crowd on the other side of the room rippled, and the rise and fall of conversation that filled the Goety and Theurgy club—better known to denizens of the Paris Otherworld as simply G&T—hushed for a few seconds.

I leaned out to look around where Carmina and Javier were craning to see who'd come in. Three men sauntered down a corridor created when the club denizens had parted, the leader a tall, dark-haired man with the brightest green eyes I'd ever seen. Two redheads followed him, all three walking with the self-assurance that said they knew exactly who they were and their place in the world. The crowd closed behind them as they approached the far end of the bar.

I smiled and, picking up my icy lemonade, pulled my purse strap over my head. "Oh yes! I'll have that, please."

"What will you have ..." Carmina's eyes widened at the same time Javier, sipping on an ale, choked and sputtered bits of ale-drenched toasted ravioli everywhere. "No! Oh, no, Guardian! You must not! That is a dragon. He is the ... what is the word, Javier?"

"Wyvern," I said in a voice that sounded remarkably like a purr. "Yummy, isn't he?"

She grabbed my arm as I slid off the stool, about to make my way over to what was obviously the fun side of G&T, her words giving me an odd sense of déjà vu. "You don't want to mess with him even if you think he could scratch the itch of your genitals. He is what my son calls bad times."

"Bad news, my love," Javier corrected her.

"Yes, that, too." Her fingers dug into my arm when I tried to move away, amused that once again I found myself in G&T, admiring the handsome green wyvern. "He is the most bad news. To cross him is to consume danger."

"I'm not afraid of him," I said, almost admitting the truth; then a mischievous urge possessed me, and although I'd often lectured my twins and Jim about giving in to the very same thing, I decided that two weeks spent parted from the dragon of my dreams meant I could indulge myself. Just a little. Just enough to remind him of what he had missed while I was back home visiting family.

"You should be," Carmina answered, but reluctantly released my arm when I took the long way around the bar that sat in the center of G&T. It didn't surprise me that packed though the club was, the people parted for me, too ... although they didn't provide as much space for me as they did Drake, Pal, and István.

I smiled at a few familiar faces coming in the door, waved at a blue dragon I recognized, and headed straight for where Drake stood at the bar, his back to me.

"Well, if it isn't Puff the Magic Dragon," I said in a voice that, while not loud, was pitched to carry.

Drake stiffened at the words, then slowly turned to face me, a glass of Dragon's Blood dangling from his long, sensitive fingers.

One glossy black eyebrow cocked. Around him, several people gasped at my apparent audacity, while a few others smiled indulgently.

"Are you, perhaps, caught in a time warp?" Drake asked, his Eastern European accent starting fires all over my body. Literally. I slapped out the flames licking my feet and ankles, and adopted what I prayed was a nonchalant saunter.

"You have something I want, Drake," I said after a moment's rummage through my memories of my first time in G&T.

His lips quirked in the way that never failed to make me weak in the knees. "I have many things you want, *kincsem*. But a gold aquamanile in the form of a dragon is sadly not one of them."

"Then I'll just have to make do with the real thing," I said, taking the glass from him and setting it on the counter before sliding my hands up his chest. He was clad in the usual suit he wore when he was in Paris—Drake had impeccable fashion sense, but he tended to be a century behind the rest of the world when it came to informal wear out in public—and I rubbed myself against him, leaning forward to say against his lips, "Perhaps I just want to role-play a little. You can be the big, bad dragon, and I'll be the feisty yet highly professional Guardian who you love beyond all reason."

Dragon fire roared to life in him as he pulled me tighter, his lips burning on mine when he growled, "I told you how much I loved you this morning, when you were waiting to leave London. I am not obliged to say it again, especially not here, in front of everyone. It is not seemly in a dragon's mate—"

I laughed out loud, so happy to see him again in person after my two weeks away that I ignored a very familiar lecture on the proper behavior of a mate in public, and instead bit his lower lip, sucked it for a second to remove the sting, then kissed him soundly before leaning to the side to say around him, "Hello, Pal. I talked to Nora this morning, and she sends her love. And, István, I like the goatee. Very dashing. Don't pay attention to anything that Jim says about it. You know how jealous it can be whenever it thinks you're outshining it."

The two men greeted me warmly, asking a few questions about our trip back home. Drake reclaimed his glass and was about to order another one for me, when I held up my lemonade. "I have one, thanks. Oh, just a second. It looks like Carmina is about to explode with concern, and she's really very sweet. A little odd, but eh. Who isn't?"

I turned when Carmina, pushing an obviously reluctant Javier in front of her, approached us.

Drake left one possessive hand on my back as I reassured Carmina that I wasn't at any risk. "We're married," I said, holding up my hand to show her the wedding ring. "So it's OK that he gets all bossy dragon on me. Well, it isn't *OK* OK, and trust me, we've had words about that, but all the same, it's nothing that I can't handle." Drake's fingers twitched on my back, but he made one of his polite bows.

Despite the fact that I wanted badly to have time alone with him, I felt it important to reassure Carmina and Javier that all was well in Aisling-land. "We arranged to meet here after I got back to Europe, but I took an earlier flight out. That's why Drake wasn't expecting me to be here. Am I babbling? I feel like I'm babbling. And man alive, am I glad Jim isn't here, because it would tell me that in an obnoxious manner."

Carmina had a bit of a glazed look about the eyes, while Javier squinted as if he was concentrating very hard. I beamed at them. "Jim's my demon, by the way. But you don't care about that. I just wanted to tell you that it's perfectly fine that Drake is standing next to me glowering."

"I am not glowering," the love of my life said in a voice tinged with martyred outrage. "I never glower. I assess in a coolly analytical and wholly glower-free manner. Also, you *are* babbling, but no one will hold that against you, since we have been parted for two weeks, and it is your way to tell me everything you've been thinking."

I decided he meant that as a compliment, and after a few more reassurances that Drake posed no threat, my handsome green-eyed dragon and I settled at a table in the corner, while István and Pal went to schmooze with friends.

Drake eyed my beverage. "Did David and Paula convert you to teetotalism while you were staying with them?"

"No, although Dad only drinks one bottle of beer after mowing the lawn, and Paula ... well, Paula is Paula. She doesn't need booze to enhance her life." I glanced around the room, but Drake's favorite table on those rare occasions when we visited Paris was suitably private. Regardless, I gave him a long look, my inner Aisling squeeing softly to itself that even after several years, Drake still had the power to make my innards turn to lust-riddled goo. "Remember that little talk we had before you went to Hungary to take care of business, and I allowed Paula and David to spoil the twins rotten?"

Drake's eyes narrowed for a moment as he thought; then suddenly he sent me a look that smoldered to the extent that the table in front of us started smoking. "You stopped your birth control?"

"You bet your scaly green tail I did." I leaned forward and licked the tip of his nose. "Paula said I shouldn't drink any alcohol just in case things happen. So it's lemonade and grapefruit juice for me until the next little dragon arrives."

For a moment, Drake's body went absolutely still, but his eyes, oh, his eyes. They were like an emerald blast furnace.

"You're trying very hard to not jump to your feet, scoop me up in your arms, and cart me off to the nearest bed to make smokin' hot dragon love to me, aren't you?" I asked.

"Yes," he answered, his voice rough with passion. "Although I would not require a bed. A strong wall would suffice. Perhaps even an unoccupied hallway if it was sufficiently dark."

I laughed again, and patted the white-knuckled hand that gripped the table. "Not that I want to dampen your libido, because I really do think it's time we enlarged our little family, but I want to talk to you before you make me mindless with pleasure."

"You are my mate," he said in that gravelly tone that hinted at the iron grip he had on his desires. "We have been parted. You know I must claim you as soon as we are reunited."

"We have been parted, but we've also FaceTimed three times a day, not to mention indulged in copious texts, and conducted numerous daily phone calls."

"The FaceTimes do not count," he said stubbornly, but I was pleased to see his fingers relaxing on the table. He glanced at his watch and added, "Those were so the children would not forget me. You may have four minutes, at which point I will either escort you home, where I can claim you as is right and proper, or I will carry you into one of Jovana's offices, pin you up against the wall, spread your legs, and—"

"Drake!" I squelched down the burble of laughter that wanted to rise. For some reason I had yet to understand, Drake was convinced that two weeks away visiting my family would erase him from the children's memory. I suspected it had a lot to do with his own mother, who frequently forgot she had two sons, and thus I didn't raise a fuss at his insecurities where the twins were concerned. "Fine, I'll subtract the chats with the kids."

He glanced around the club. "They are at home?"

"Of course. They were just going down for their naps because we decided to fly rather than take the train. Iarlaith was happy to play with his tablet, but Ilona was a wild beast and would not settle on the flight from Seattle to London." I lifted my brows. "She's very much your child."

Drake, who never saw much use for modesty, attempted now to don a modest expression. It failed miserably. "They carry my nature. It is the way of dragonkin."

"Uh-huh. Well, let's have a little chat before we return home and let your mini-me hellions tell you all about the octopus they freed from the Seattle Aquarium, and why we are banned from ever returning there. Has something been going on here? In Paris, I mean."

"I have been in Paris exactly forty-seven minutes. If there is, I have had little time to be made aware of it. What has you concerned?" he asked, his fingers now stroking mine in a way that reminded me the clock was ticking and I had three minutes left before I would (happily, and with ecstasy) allow him to carry me off home, where we could reacquaint ourselves with the steamy lovemaking abilities of dragons.

"First, the guy at passport control just about had a meltdown when he saw my name on my passport, and ran off muttering that the end was nigh. Then Rene wasn't around to drive us, and you know Rene always finds us when we're in Paris. And lastly, Carmina and Javier mentioned something about an influx of imps as well as what I gather is a general sense of things not being right, and you know how both of those can be a portent of trouble."

"Hmm," Drake said, pausing in the finger stroking to consider the information. "That all seems rather nebulous, but I will call Kostya if you like. Until last week, he was in Paris for the last few months."

I smiled at him and stood up, brushing down my gauzy sundress, and reveling in the approving way Drake's gaze crawled over it. "Maybe call him after we get home and have some quality time together."

"It shall be as you like," he said, getting to his feet with a very lascivious look in his eye, one that sent little shivers down my spine. "Perhaps a bath is in order, as well."

I thought of Drake reclining seductively in his massively oversized tub, his body slick and warm with bath oil. I thought of how much I wanted to touch all those slippery expanses of flesh, and what I would do to him. Then I dwelt on what he'd do to me, and the next thing I knew, I was running for the door.

He beat me to it, his passion so great that a scorched imprint of his hand was left on the door as we raced out into the street.

* * *

It took a full two months before I could pinpoint what it was that was making me uneasy. "It's all the imps, Nora," I said into my phone, watching absently as the children romped in the tiny garden space that came with Drake's Paris house. "I would have thought the couple in G&T were exaggerating, but since we've been home, I've seen seven different imps out in public. And you know the little buggers seldom hang out in open spaces."

"That is very unusual," Nora agreed. She hesitated a moment, then added, "I have not noticed any undue activity here in London, nor have I heard anything from the guild about an influx. We get such things at Vexamen, of course, but that is not pertinent to this situation."

"Vexamen? I'm so glad Jim isn't here, because it would give me endless grief for what I'm about to ask, but what exactly is that?" I asked, the word sounding familiar, but I was distracted by keeping an eye on the kids as they splashed in a wading pool, and couldn't pull the definition to mind.

"It is the time of upheaval in Abaddon. You were not a Guardian when the last one happened?"

"I don't think so, no," I answered, ignoring when the twins threw grass into their blow-up pool.

"Ah, well, in a nutshell, Bael should have stepped down from his position of premiere prince, which meant the other princes would have fought for the job, but Bael is ... well, Bael. He did not step down."

"That definitely sounds like it was before my time. Interesting. And there were lots of imps then?" I asked, relieved to know that Bael was now safely contained in the Akasha.

"Not during Vexamen per se, but during Salvaticus, which occurs before it. It is the time of rebirth for revenants, and imps seem to use that as an excuse to pour into the mortal world. But we will not have another Vexamen for, oh, many centuries."

"Well, it's got me beat why the imps are everywhere. I know they come out when the dragons are warring, but everything is peachy keen in the weyr. Oh, there's Drake. He looks a bit smoky about the nostrils, so I'd better go see what has riled him up. If you hear anything, let me know, OK?"

"Absolutely. My best to you all."

"Likewise." I hung up, greeted the nanny Grace, who followed on Drake's heels, and gave her swift instructions about watching the children. "They can have another ten minutes splashing about—Iarlaith! We do not take our swimsuit off and hit our sister on the head with it. But then they'll need sunscreen again, and if they insist on having naked time in the wading pool, don't let them go over to the far side of the garden where people can see through the fence. All right, munchkins! Grace is in charge until it's time for lunch."

The twins cheered, and immediately starting slapping each other with their wet swimsuits. I looked at Drake.

He watched them with pursed lips for a moment, saying merely, "All green dragons prefer to be in the water without the constriction of clothing."

"Uh-huh. Why do I have a feeling you encourage that behavior when I'm not looking?"

He tried very hard to arrange an innocent expression on his face, but failed miserably.

I took his hand and returned into the house with him, asking, "Did you get hold of Kostya?"

"I didn't have to." He opened the door to his study. A tall, dark, and intensely scowling man paced past the door, his hands clasped behind his back.

"So I see. Hello, Kostya. What brings you to Paris?"

"Baltic, naturally." Kostya said something profane, then continued, "As ever, he brings nothing but grief to the dragonkin and weyr."

"Baltic? He's with Ysolde in Dauva. She's going to have her baby soon, and there's no way he'd leave her. Wait, you're not still bitching because he's so close to your home in Saint Petersburg, are you?" I asked, curling up next to Drake when he sat on the couch. Kostya never lost the opportunity to complain about what he deemed an ulterior motive for Baltic reclaiming his home in Latvia.

"I don't bitch! I'm a wyvern! Wyverns don't bitch!" he said (in a bitchy voice), storming past me trailing dragon fire. Luckily, our carpets are fireproof. "If I complain—righteously and in an extremely justified, masculine manner—then it is because once again we are left to clean up after Baltic's blunders."

"What blunder?" I asked Drake, knowing that I'd get a more understandable answer from him.

"Thala," Drake said, his hands teasing the hairs at the back of my neck as I slid him a look that warned I wouldn't be able to stand much without jumping him.

"Oh, her." I wondered if Kostya was here for any particular reason other than complaining to his brother, or if there was a chance I could hustle him out of the house and get Drake into the basement, where he had a pool that we both greatly enjoyed.

"Oh, her? *Oh, her*?" Kostya struck his usual dramatic manner, one hand waving in the air. "You speak of her as if she is nothing but an inconvenience, but because Baltic couldn't hold on to the mage sword Antonia von Endres had given him, now we must clean up his mess and find Thala."

"Huh?" I stopped thinking about exploring naked time with Drake, and turned around to look at Kostya. "What are you talking about?"

Drake looked annoyed. "Dr. Kostich, apparently, has sent word to Ysolde as the weyr representative that since the sword was held by dragons—"

"Stolen by Drake, I believe, were his words," Kostya said with a look at his brother.

"Since the sword was held by dragons when it was stolen by Baltic's former lieutenant, then it falls to the dragonkin to reclaim it."

"That's just bull," I said, getting annoyed right along with Drake. "Didn't Dr. Kostich make some big song and dance about it belonging to mages, and thus they would find it?"

"They haven't been able to locate Thala," Kostya said, pacing past us again. "Thus he has seen fit to blame us for the mages' incompetence, and insist that we locate and return the sword, or pay."

"Pay what?" I asked, a little ball of worry forming in my stomach. "Surely the sword is priceless. He can't expect us to pay for something that's priceless."

"He's not asking for payment in coin, *kincsem*," Drake said, his fingers still stroking the back of my neck. Drake was never one for public shows of affection, but I knew by the way his fire was simmering inside of him that he, too, was thinking of the pool. "Evidently he told Ysolde that if the weyr does not produce the sword, our agreement with the L'au-dela will be broken, and we will be considered outsiders."

I blinked a couple of times at the audacity of the man. "He's out of his ever-lovin' mind."

Kostya snorted, and stomped back across the room to the fireplace. "That is the biggest understatement I have heard. He is mad if he thinks to blame us because his mages cannot catch one simple half-dragon."

"Thala is many things," I said slowly, digging through my memories to what I knew about her. "But she's a dirge singer, and the daughter of an archimage and a dragon. I don't think simple is a word one could use about her. OK. So, being kicked out of the L'au-dela is not an option."

"Technically we are not in it," Drake pointed out while Kostya muttered a few more rude things about Dr. Kostich. "But it would void our agreement with them, and that is an event I am loath to see happen. Especially now."

"I agree in general, but why now in particular?" I asked. "You mean because of all the imps?"

"That and . . ." Drake was silent for a moment, his gaze on Kostya, who had stopped pacing, and was wearing an almost identical expression of introspection. "I believe I was too hasty to dismiss your misgivings two months ago, Aisling."

"There's a rumor that some dragons have been seen in Paris," Kostya said slowly, meeting Drake's gaze.

"So? There's lots of dragons here, of all the septs." I waited for them to spill and, when they weren't immediately forthcoming, nudged Drake. "What's so important about these dragons that it brought Kostya all the way from Saint Petersburg?"

"I'm not absolutely certain they are dragons," Drake said. "The report we've had is that they are somehow . . . tainted."

A cold chill skittered down my spine. It wasn't Drake's words so much as the worry evident in them that gave me a bad feeling.

A very bad feeling.

My dear Friia,

I have not intentionally "teased" you, as you claim in your latest electronic message. It has been a very long time since any of my siblings have expressed anything beyond a mild interest in the dragonkin, but since you wish to know more about the peril hanging over my descendants, I will naturally acquiesce to your wishes for further information.

At the moment, the biggest threat to my children is that one of the lords of Abaddon is muddying the waters with his attempt at revenge. It is distracting dragons when they should be looking to the true foe.

Your devoted brother,
First Dragon

TWO

KOSTYA DOES PARIS

Konstantin Fekete was not in a good mood. "I am not in a good mood," he informed Piotr, his newly appointed lieutenant and guard.

Piotr looked duly impressed by this news, a fact that both mollified and annoyed Kostya. He disliked yes-men, but at the same time, he was a wyvern, and his feelings, thoughts, and desires should be of utmost importance to the members of his sept.

That thought lasted a few seconds until he realized that although he had many flaws, conceit was not one of them, and he had no intention of indulging in it now.

He sighed, and glanced across the car to where Piotr sat facing him. "I apologize. It is not your problem if I am not in a good mood."

Piotr looked downright confused. "It's not? But—you are wyvern."

"Yes. But a good wyvern thinks of the sept, not of himself," he said, the lessons learned over the centuries slowly returning to him. "Thus, my foul mood at the news that we, once again, must clean up after the madman who all but wiped us from the face of the earth is not a matter for you to worry about."

"Erm ..." Piotr looked even more confused than a few seconds ago. "The madman who wiped us from the earth? Bael?"

"No. Baltic!" Kostya bit back an oath, well aware that his new guard was a youngster, not even a hundred years old, born into hiding, and only in recent years gathered back into the bosom of the sept. "Baltic is the one who destroyed us. Or tried to. He had help from others, notably that bastard Constantine and his silver traitors, but most of the blame falls squarely on Baltic. Which is why I cut him down."

"Baltic's alive," Piotr pointed out, and it was at that moment that Kostya realized that not only was his new lieutenant unlearned in dragon lore; he was also not the brightest pea in the split pea soup.

He gave a mental sigh this time. It was just his luck that his sept, his beloved black dragons, was filled with younglings. Naive younglings. "Make a note. Just as soon as we prove or disprove the rumors about tainted dragons, we are going to start a series of educational classes for the sept on its glorious history and near demise."

Piotr hastily made some notes on his phone. At least, Kostya thought to himself, looking out the window as the glittering lights of Paris flashed by, the lad was eager to work.

That thought stayed with him until they approached *Le Simulacre*, the nightclub where it was whispered that a curious new form of red dragon had been seen recently. "Be on your guard," Kostya told Piotr as the two emerged from the car. "Do not reveal information—gather only. Remember that you are a member of one of the original four septs, and do not allow others to intimidate you."

Piotr's Adam's apple bobbed, but he nodded. Kostya had a moment of disquietude about bringing the young dragon into what might be a dangerous situation, but just made a mental note that he would have to see to his protection should there be trouble.

Drake and Aisling were already inside, Drake in the act of forcing his mate into a corner booth.

"—and as I have mentioned far too often, it is not appropriate for you to argue with me when it comes to your welfare," he said, looking annoyed with his mate.

Kostya smirked to himself. Someday, when he found a mate, she would be mindful of who he was, and what respect was owed to him. She would not behave in the manner that Aisling did with regard to Drake. Or for that matter, the silver mate. More than once, he had heard May contradict Gabriel, something that still surprised Kostya. And then there was Ysolde … but he checked that thought before it could even continue, well aware that Ysolde belonged in a class to herself when it came to mates. His long history with her was sadly not what it should be, since she often treated him with the mild annoyance of one who was dealing with a particularly pesky younger brother.

"And I told you that if you want me to light your hair on fire right here in front of everyone, just keep up the bossy act. I'm only *just* pregnant, Drake. Just barely, so tell those protective instincts that I know are charging around inside of your fabulous body to chill. They can go into overtime later, once you have to help me get out of chairs," Aisling answered Drake, giving him a look that secretly shocked Kostya.

Although he was the older brother, Kostya had a healthy respect for Drake, and knew well just how swift could be his anger once his temper snapped. That Aisling was apparently unafraid of him spoke much of their affection, and for a moment, an oddly hollow sense gripped Kostya. Normally not one for indulging in introspective moments, he allowed his attention to turn inward, surprised to find that the feeling resolved itself into a sense of longing.

He wanted to be looked at the way Aisling was looking at Drake. More, he wanted a woman in his life to whom he could devote himself, one who needed him. One whom he could protect and cherish, and who would always have his back the way Aisling always had Drake's. In short, he wanted a mate.

That realization made him feel hotly uncomfortable, which resulted in him saying irritably, "If you two are done arguing, perhaps we can get down to business."

Aisling turned a look on him, eyeing his hair in a manner that spoke volumes. He ran a hand over it to make sure it wasn't on fire before he realized what he was doing, deepening his sense of aggrievement.

"Spoken like a man who doesn't know the difference between a discussion between a husband and wife, and people having an argument. Yes, Drake, I'm sitting down now, but not because I'm going to break if I don't do so, but because I wore heels and for some reason, they're pinching my pinkie toes. Is that who I think it is?"

Kostya turned in the direction that Aisling nodded, noting the woman with a short blond pageboy haircut who stood chatting with two men he recognized as thief takers. Behind her, a tall man with a gaunt face pushed through the crowd to join her.

"It is interesting, is it not, that both Jovana and the archimage should be at this club at the very same time we are?" Kostya said, his gaze on the small group of people. "Do you think they have heard the rumors of the red dragons, too?"

"It is doubtful," Drake answered, watching the group, as well, before sliding into the circular booth next to Aisling. "Kostich has an aversion to dragonkin despite his granddaughter being ouroboros."

"Dr. Kostich is here?" Aisling made a face. "Great. Just what we need to put a damper on our evening out. Right, I want to hear what's up with the red sept."

"Now is not the time," Drake started to say, but Aisling shot him another of the looks that Kostya thought might push his brother over the edge.

"You promised to explain what rumors you've heard once we were here," she interrupted. "Do you think these bad dragons are from the red sept? And why did you say you thought the red dragons might not be dragons? What else would they be if not dragons?"

Drake was silent for a few moments, his brow furrowed. Kostya said, "One of the members of my sept—a woman named Helene Two Feathers—was in Paris a few days ago, and said she saw a group of three red dragons in one of the parks. She said they looked like dragons, but once she got close, they bore the stench of Abaddon."

"Demon smoke, you mean?" Aisling asked, looking thoughtful. "So they were around demons?"

"Not around them," Drake answered her with a glance at Kostya. "The black dragon said she thought they were demons. Or rather, some sort of a hybrid."

"No," Aisling said, shaking her head. "How can that be? Dragons can't be demons. You can't even summon them."

"They were hybrids," Kostya said with distaste. "Foul ones."

"How on earth can a dragon also be a demon?" Aisling asked, looking horrified and confused at the same time.

"We don't know," Kostya said simply. "No one else has seen those three red dragons, so we have little information other than what Helene saw."

"She must have been mistaken," Aisling said after another moment's reflection. "I know demons, and there's no way that demons and dragons can mix. Maybe it's a demon using a glamour, or someone else pulling a truly epic-level joke, but I just can't believe there are demonic dragons. No. It's a joke. It has to be."

Kostya said nothing while Aisling continued to dismiss the idea. Judging by the worried expression Drake slipped him, neither of them was inclined to point out that Aisling was far off base with her assessment of what was real, and what was a deception.

"Oooh, Drake," she said after a few minutes of chat. "There's a band setting up. Live music! We can dance before we have to mingle with Dr. Kostich and Jovana, and see what they know about someone who can pull off the sort of glamour that would make everyone believe there were dragon hybrids running around."

"We do not dance in public," he told her sternly.

"But you're such a good dancer. You make even me with my two left feet look good."

Drake gave her a look that Kostya would not like to have received. "You just announced that your feet were hurting. Dancing would not be comfortable for you."

"Pfft," Aisling said, kicking off her shoes and sliding out of the booth. "I'm an old hand at dancing barefoot. Come on. One quick dance before we start working the crowd and see what people know about someone with a super glamour."

"Kincsem, I just told you—" Drake heaved a martyred sigh and, without meeting Kostya's eye, slid out and followed Aisling to the dance floor set at the far end of the club. He paused long enough to say softly, "Keep an eye on Kostich just in case he is up to something."

"Dr. Kostich is the head of the Committee, is he not?" Piotr asked, his voice pitched for Kostya's ears alone. "Why would the green wyvern believe he is up to something?"

"Because he usually is. And *that* is exactly why both he and the Venediger are here," Kostya said in response to the group that came down the stairs into the club proper. Music now throbbed from the band, who had just started an uninspired dance tune, while the air, redolent of the scents of so many Otherworld denizens crammed into a small space, seemed to thicken with anticipation.

"What?" Piotr examined the group. "The woman? She is a dragon, is she not?"

"Her father was," Kostya said softly, watching as Thala paused at the bottom of the stairs. "But she is no mere dragon. For one, she worked with Fiat Blu to kill numerous blue dragons. For another, she stole a sword that has value to mages. Beyond that, I find it surprising that she is here now. Surprising and that she is in Paris at the same time as the dragon hybrids. Quickly—go tell Drake that Thala is here."

He started to move toward the woman and two men as they merged into the crowd of people who filled the spaces between the central bar and the walls while chatting, laughing, drinking, and, in some cases, indulging in mild sexual foreplay, and paused only when Piotr asked, "Thala?"

"For the love of the saints!" Kostya snarled under his breath, not taking his gaze off the redheaded necromancer who had been the cause of so much trouble to the dragonkin. "Do you hear nothing I tell you? Thala was Baltic's lieutenant. She stole a valuable mage sword from him, which explains why two of the most powerful people in the Otherworld are waiting here. Now go warn my brother, and when you have done so, go around the other side to flank Thala."

Kostya moved through the crowd, heading toward his target, wishing that Drake's two bodyguards hadn't been sent away to investigate a rumor about the red dragons being seen in London. He had faith in his abilities as well as Drake's, but of Piotr he was less certain, and from what he'd been told about Thala, she had skills that could well prove lethal if she was not captured quickly.

He had maneuvered himself behind her and what he assumed were her two guards, when a flicker at the right side of his peripheral vision had him momentarily distracted.

Two male dragons had reached the bottom of the stairs and spotted him.

Not dragons, he mentally corrected himself, but some sort of horrible parody of a dragon. The foul stench of demonic beings reached his nostrils at the same time the two dragons—red dragons—launched themselves at him. Helene had been correct—these were dragons who had changed on a fundamental level. They were neither dragon nor demon, but some obscene mixture of both.

Thala and entourage spun around at the screech of anger from the red dragon demons. Despite the shaded lighting of that section of the club, he caught the glint of metal in their hands, and he instantly shifted into dragon form, lashing out at the attackers with a spinning kick followed by a tail slap.

The nearest dragon stabbed Kostya's thigh with a long curved dagger, but the second hybrid caught the force of Kostya's kick dead in the chest and went flying backward, impaling himself on a wrought iron spindle decorating the staircase. Immediately, the dragon dissolved into an oily black smoke, but Kostya had no time to do more than enjoy a fleeting moment of satisfaction before the second dragon was upon him again, this time slashing across his upper arm.

"Dragons!" Thala raised her hand, a blue-white ball of arcane power forming. For a moment, Kostya had hopes that she was talking about the demonic red dragon, but that hope died when she flung the ball at him. He only just ducked in time, slashing out again with tail and claws, this time catching the attacking dragon monstrosity.

Across the thump of the music, he could hear a couple of muffled shouts, and suddenly, the music stopped, and the occupants of the club bolted.

"It never fails—" He grunted when the red dragon demon kicked him in the gut, sending him flying backward a few yards to slam against a wall. He was on his feet before his attacker could disembowel him, but it was a near thing. "—to amaze me how—"

Piotr appeared out of nowhere and flung himself onto the back of the demon, stabbing at his neck with a short dagger. The demon screamed, and spun around, Piotr still clinging to his back.

"—they can get out without trampling anyone. Drake! The red demons are here!" Kostya, snatching up the dead dragon's sword, jammed it deep into the remaining demon's chest before leaping forward to take a flying tackle at Thala. Although he would have preferred to keep one of the hybrids alive for questioning, the opportunity to capture the woman who was responsible for the deaths of so many dragons was impossible to ignore.

Unfortunately, he missed her when she spun out of the way. She snarled something obscene and cast up her hands, a low droning noise coming from her mouth while her two guards stood in front of her, clearly hoping to provide a protective shield.

"She's singing a dirge!" a woman cried, and Kostya had a brief glimpse of the Venediger Jovana before Dr. Kostich pushed before her, his hands dancing in the air. "Silence her!"

Kostya wasn't about to risk her finishing the song that was rooted in dark earth magic, the kind that knew only death and destruction. He saw Drake running toward him from behind Thala, and flung himself forward, shifting his dragon form to human just as Thala's guards braced for his descent.

The look on their faces when his much slimmer human form sailed between them was priceless enough to tuck away for enjoyment later. What wasn't enjoyable was the crackle of dark power that Thala slammed into him just as he was about to grab her, knocking him back into her guards with such force that they slid halfway across the club.

"You dare!" Thala almost spat the words at him, stopping the terrible noise of the dirge in order to revile him. "I will not tolerate this! You are nothing. Less than nothing, and so shall you return to the earth." Words as sharp as daggers flew from her mouth, tearing into Kostya's flesh.

"I wonder how Baltic tolerated you as long as he did," Kostya managed to say, getting painfully to his feet. He had a suspicion that not only were a couple of his ribs broken, but his collarbone, as well. "Luckily, I don't have to stand here and listen to you."

Thala's eyes glowed a brown red, but Kostya had done his job—he'd distracted her enough for Dr. Kostich and Drake to work their way through the fleeing patrons until they were directly behind her.

"What—" She spun around just as Dr. Kostich, whose hands had been dancing in the air creating a physical spell, flung wide his hands and cast it upon her, locking her to the ground. Drake quickly ripped off his tie and jerked Thala's hands behind her, tying them.

"You fools," Thala said, now looking at Jovana and Dr. Kostich. "Do you think I did not know this was a trap? Do you think I am not able to bring down this building upon you? I will level this entire city before I—"

Kostya, who had been limping forward while tearing off one sleeve of his shirt, reached behind Thala and, with a quick move that sent shards of pain deep inside his chest, gagged her. "That's better. And now I'll take this."

He thought for a moment that Thala's head might explode with rage when he jerked a small leather pouch that hung from a chain around her neck, pulling from it a small blue crystal. The famed mage sword of Antonia von Endres might not look like anything in its dormant state, but he knew it was the most valuable talisman of magedom.

"Give that to me!" Dr. Kostich bellowed, storming around a madly struggling Thala, who was immediately hoisted by four men, no doubt to take her off to a place of imprisonment. "That belongs to mages, not to dragons."

"It's mine now," Kostya said with a complacence that he was far from feeling. He hurt everywhere, and although he could see that Piotr was still alive, the red dragon demon had done great damage to him.

"We'll see about that," snapped Kostich, and his hands started moving in the air again.

"Hey!" Aisling said, her voice filled with warning. "You can't do that! It's against the terms of the weyr agreement!"

Kostich interrupted her with an invective that had her spitting little balls of fire at him. "The sword belongs to mages!"

"It belongs to whoever holds it, and that's me," Kostya corrected, and would have continued, but at that moment the door at the top of the stairs was flung open, and a stream of red demon dragons poured into the club.

"Give me the sword," Jovana cried, running forward, one of her hands drawing protective wards. The other she held out toward Kostya.

He hesitated for a moment, his gaze moving between the dragons that raced down the stairs to him, flickering over to where Drake stood protectively in front of Aisling.

"I can use it," Jovana snapped, gesturing impatiently. "You can't!"

With only a morsel of regret, he tossed her the crystal, running back to the dead dragon to pull from his chest the sword he'd used earlier. Piotr, covered in blood and sweat, and with an arm that was clearly broken, staggered forward with the other sword. Kostya gave him a nod of approval, and turned to face the onslaught, ignoring the agony of his shoulder and ribs.

He had to admit later that Jovana wielded the mage sword well. It positively sang as it beheaded, maimed, and disemboweled the attacking demonic-dragon hybrids. Drake, who managed to take a morning star and a small ax from a pair of dragons that Jovana had decapitated, leaped into the fray with a cry that Kostya remembered from his youth. Kostich moved behind them, arcane blasts exploding with brilliant blue-white light that flashed like an overpowered strobe, leaving Kostya with black spots before his eyes.

Well behind them, standing on top of a table, Aisling cast wards on any of the demon red dragons that made it past Kostya, Drake, and the mages.

The pain started to overwhelm Kostya. He had shifted into dragon form several times, drawing on the strength inherent in his primal being, but after what seemed an eternity, the injuries started to catch up with him. Piotr had long since retreated to stand with Aisling, but was now crumpled on a booth seat, blood streaming to the floor. Kostya had no time to do more than make sure Piotr was alive before he continued defending the club from the attackers.

Just as the inky spots began to clump together and partially blind him, the wave thinned to a trickle of dragons. By the time the last one had been dispatched, he knew he was very close to passing out. "What Helene said …" He staggered a few steps to the side when he tried to reach Drake. "… was true. Those were demons."

"Not demons. But not dragons," Drake said, sweat and blood streaking his face. He glanced back to check on Aisling, who gave him a weary smile before turning to Piotr with a damp cloth. "Your description of hybrid seems to be apt, as they are definitely a mix of both."

"Dragon hunters," Dr. Kostich snarled, his voice rough from invoking the verbal element of the spells. He, too, was covered in sweat and blood, but he had enough energy to give both Drake and Kostya a foul look.

"No," Drake said, shaking his head. "Dragon hunters do not let their demon side take control. These were something else. Something … evil."

"Whatever they are, they had their origin in the red sept," Kostya said, meeting his brother's gaze. "Which makes me wonder just where Jian is."

"If they are dragonkin, then I expect you to resolve the issue of their existence," Dr. Kostich said, his voice as sharp as a razor. "I will not have them attacking the L'au-dela."

Kostya eyed him for a few seconds, too tired to even feel enraged by such an outrageous slander. "They aren't dragonkin, as my brother just said. They are other."

"Something needs to be done with them," Jovana said, watching as a few of her entourage limped up the stairs to make sure the street was clear. She hesitated a second, looking at the crystal in her hand, the mage sword having returned to its quiescent state. "You yielded this sword to me in a time of need, but I am no thief. This is a relic of magedom, however, and I would ask that you grant its care to me."

"Jovana!" Dr. Kostich sounded as outraged as he looked. "The sword is ours! You need not ask permission to keep what can only be used by a mage. Dragonkin, with the exception of that behemoth Baltic, cannot use it. They wish to hold it just as they hold every other valuable—because they can."

She ignored him, meeting Kostya's gaze. He noted that she looked a bit battered, but had obviously fared better than any of the rest of the front line. He studied her face for a moment, then shifted his gaze to Drake. Drake frowned, grimaced, then, with a slight shrug, nodded.

"Very well," Kostya said, too weary to really care what happened to the blighted thing. There was a slight satisfaction in knowing that it would enrage Baltic to know the sword had been returned to the mages, but true enjoyment of that fact would have to wait until such time as he healed up. "Keep it safe, Venediger."

A ghost of a smile passed over her lips as she tucked the crystal away. "You may rest assured that I will do so, dragon."

"What are we going to do now?" Aisling asked a little while later, as they stood outside the club, waiting for their respective cars.

"Go home, and heal," Drake said, wincing as he flexed a swollen hand.

"And the red demon dudes?" she asked, looking from him to Kostya, who wanted nothing more than to pour himself into bed, and sleep for approximately half a year.

Silence settled around them.

"We will contact Jian," Drake said finally. "He must have the answers we seek."

Kostya had a premonition that it wasn't going to be quite that simple.

My dear Friia,

I would express surprise regarding the language of your latest message, but then I remembered to whom you are married, and all was made clear.

Despite your accusations, I have been forthcoming with information. Plainly stated, the dragonkin are in peril. In addition to that, one of the lords of Abaddon has seen fit to meddle with them.

A word in the ear of one of his minions will hopefully make my children realize the truth of what is happening.

Your devoted brother despite the allegations of withholding "the good details,"

First Dragon

THREE

DIARY OF EFFRIJIM, DEMON SIXTH CLASS, AND ALL-AROUND STUDMUFFIN

Day 584,171

The day started out well. I mean, how can you find fault in a morning spent lying in the sunshine in the garden of a French cottage, your beloved by your side, gently snoring and twitching while she dreams? Yeah, nothing beats that, especially when your beloved's dog mom, Amelie, trots out to the garden with a tray filled with noms.

"Jim, no! You had your breakfast," Amelie scolded when I left the patch of morning sun and ambled over to see what she had under the starched white cloth covering a tray. "This is mine."

"Yeah, but Cecile and I had a long walk around the garden already, and what with all the walks you make me go on, I've got to be dropping weight like mad. You don't want me to end up nothing but skin and bones, do you? Oooh, croissants? Is that from the boulangerie down the road, the one with the *pains au chocolat*?"

"Chocolate is poisonous to dogs, as you well know," Amelie said, slapping at my nose when I tried to ascertain what type of croissant it was. "Jim, I said no! Croissants are not on the list of foods that Aisling said you may eat."

"Bah. She's been brainwashed by some deranged vet who worries way too much about cholesterol. Have you ever heard of a dog having high cholesterol? Me either. It's madness, Amelie, pure madness, and oh, since I seem to have gotten a bit of drool on that croissant right at the edge of your plate, I'll just eat it, shall I?"

"Jim!" she repeated in a dismayed tone, but I knew the truth. She loved me almost as much as Ash did. "What I will tell Aisling when I take you home is beyond the understanding. No, you may not have jam with the croissant you conveniently set upon with your lips. Are your things packed? We will leave after we have our morning promenade around the town."

"Yeah, I'm packed, although if you wanted to spend another week out here, I wouldn't mind."

She paused in the act of sipping coffee, her brows a little pulled together. "I have never known you to not wish to return home at the end of one of our delightful holidays. Is something wrong between you and the green dragons? Do you fear the lecture of Aisling when she sees that you have gained the pounds rather than have lost them?"

"I'm as fit as I ever was, what with all the walkies we take. Hey, speaking of that, can you put a blanket in that kids' wagon that I found in the shed yesterday? Cecile might like to ride in that when we go for our walk. I'd pull it if you liked. Her legs are so short, you know. Those walks are a bit tough on her."

Amelie stared at me for a moment, then gave a moist sniff, and to my surprise—mortals, man, you just never know with them—leaned down and kissed the top of my head before offering me half a croissant. One without jam, I couldn't help but notice. "Jim, just when I begin to question why I spend so much time catering to a demon, you say something that makes me believe in the goodness of all beings. Yes, I, too, have noticed that Cecile is slowing down on our walks, and I was intending on buying her a pram when we returned to Paris, but for today, you may pull the wagon, and she will ride like a princess in a palanquin."

It's while we were out for our walkies, with Amelie having rigged together two leashes onto the wagon as a sort of harness—I wouldn't do this for anyone but my beloved fuzzybutt—that Aisling called.

"Yeah, babe, I'm here," I said when Amelie put the phone on speaker. "Amelie says we should be back in Paris by dinnertime, so be sure to tell Suzanne that I'll be starving and will need extra food to compensate for all the exercise Amelie's been making me take. Whoa. Don't rock the wagon, Cecile. I'm not exactly a horse."

"You're not a what?" Aisling asked, then hurried on before I could answer. "Never mind, it doesn't matter. I have an odd sort of question to ask you both."

"OK," I said, marching along the lane, ignoring all the tantalizing smells coming from the hedge. I didn't want to upset Cecile, who had just snuggled back down into the blanket nest that Amelie had made for her. "I'm all over odd, girlfriend. What's up?"

"It's two somethings, actually. First of all, do you know anything about some red dragons having been imbued with demonic beings?"

"What? Man, Ash, are you at the crack pipe again? There ain't no such thing as a demon who is also a dragon. I mean, other than dragon hunters, but those dudes are something different altogether."

"A what, now? No, never mind, just answer the quest. Have you heard anything about the red dragons?"

"Nope. Not a word. Mind you, we don't get a lot of dragon chatter out here," I pointed out.

"That is so," Amelie said, turning us around so we were heading back toward our temporary home. "I, myself, have heard nothing from the Otherworld."

She sighed. "I thought that would be the case. The second thing is a bit more intangible. It's probably a moot point if you guys aren't getting any of the rumor mill out there, but ... it's a feeling I have that I just can't account for. Have either of you heard about something ..." She hesitated a moment. "It's hard to pinpoint, but basically something dangerous in the offing?"

"Dangerous? No, I have not heard anything like that," Amelie said at the same time I answered, "You mean that thing about Asmodeus sending his legions out into the wild looking for a ring? Other than that, nope, everything's copacetic."

"Jim!" Amelie said again in the same outraged tone she is wont to use around me. Aisling said the same thing in almost the same tone, although she added quite a few swear words after her initial exclamation.

"I hope you haven't been using that sort of language around the spawn," I told Aisling once she sputtered to a stop. "You know how fast they pick up things."

"Yes, and the next time you go around muttering the words to a spell that causes profound flatulence, I will banish you for a whole month to the Akasha. Poor István still gets twitchy whenever he's alone with the twins."

I may have snickered at that. István also loves me—he just likes to hide it behind a lot of dirty looks and muttered imprecations. And sometimes he takes my

Welsh Corgi Fancier magazines, but I bet that's just because he can't resist the fuzzybutts, too.

"What is this?" Amelie asked, her face all scrunched up with worry. "There is a legion of demons sent to look for a ring? What ring? For what purpose? Aisling, you must speak with the Guardians' Guild about this."

"You bet your sweet bippy I will," Aisling promised. "Jim, how did you hear about this? And for the love of all that's green and scaly, why didn't you tell me there was a legion of demons roaming around the Otherworld?"

"I heard about it from Mehet, an old buddy from Abaddon who went dybbuk from Sally—May's friend, you remember her?—and who hit me up on LinkedIn as a personal reference."

"I … of course I remember Sally. … LinkedIn? Demons use LinkedIn?" Aisling seemed to have a hard time with that idea.

"We're demons, not savages, Ash. We use LinkedIn, and Tinder, and WhatsApp, and that mobile game that's like Scrabble, but it's not, and you can make up dirty words to get extra points." I gave Cecile a roll of my eyes to express just how silly humans can be, but she was snoring away on her bed of blankies, and I hate disturbing her when she's snoozing. She gets a bit snappy if you wake her up.

The sound of someone taking several deep breaths followed, after which Aisling said, "Amelie, do you happen to have a rolled-up newspaper or magazine handy? Something with which you can whomp Jim on the head?"

Amelie made a little face of regret. "No, I'm afraid I do not have anything of that sort," she answered.

"Hey!" I said, watching her closely, just in case she suddenly found something whomp-worthy. "It's not cool trying to drag Amelie into your demon-abusing ways. Besides, she kissed me on my head this morning. You can't kiss me one minute and wallop me with a magazine the next."

"Why are the demons in the mortal world looking for a ring?" Aisling asked, the words sounding like they were spoken through gritted teeth. "Asmodeus is the premiere prince—what's so special about this ring that he needs it when he's plenty powerful on his own? And most of all, why didn't you tell me this was going on?"

"I didn't tell you because you were in the US showing off the spawn to your family, and also, because you didn't ask me."

"I'm asking you now," she said in an overly dramatic voice.

"Yeah, but you weren't before," I pointed out helpfully, adding sotto voce to Amelie, "Aisling has mom brains. The spawn wear down her normal intelligence cells and leave her a bit scattered."

"I do not have mom brains!" Aisling all but shouted in the phone, then immediately added (thankfully, at a lower volume), "Well, I do, but that's only because I am a mother, and I worry about my children. And part of that worry is focused on their well-being, something that is at risk if there are demons running hither and yon. What do the demons hope to do with this ring?"

"Do I look like the demon form of Google?" I rolled my eyes again, but Amelie was too busy taking charge of the wagon, unhooking me, and marching double time back to her little country cottage to notice. I followed behind, talking into the phone, which rested in the wagon next to Cecile. "I don't know every demon just because I've been around a few years."

"You're over twelve hundred years old, and don't sidestep my questions."

"Oh sure, just yell out how old I am where anyone can hear. You know how sensitive I am about my age," I told her with a martyred sniff.

There was another "taking several deep breaths" sort of noise.

"Effrijim, I command thee to answer my friggin' questions and stop being a twit!"

I sighed heavily, because seriously, did any other demon have to put up with such behavior? "I told you that I don't know what the demons are doing other than Mehet said something about a ring, and Asmodeus wanting to lay down a curse now that His Unholy Jerkface has been banished to the Akasha."

"Unholy Jerk—oh, Bael? Wait, what curse?"

"Mehet didn't say. He just asked me for a reference, said Asmo was looking for a ring, and planning some big curse."

"Hmm." Aisling clearly thought about that while we walked quickly back to the cottage. I gave Cecile's ears a few swipes of the ole tongue just because. "That doesn't make any sense. Why would Asmodeus need a ring to cast a curse? And who is he planning on cursing?"

"Dunno, except ..." It was my turn to be thoughtful.

"Except what?" Aisling demanded.

I waited until Amelie carried Cecile into the house. "It may be nothing. ..."

"Jim, so help me—"

"Yeah, yeah, you'll send me to the Akasha. Like that's anything new? I got the Hashmallim's numbers now, babe."

"You do not. Except what?"

I sighed again. Sometimes, it was hard work following the rules of demonhood. "Except there had to be a reason Mehet told me about it."

Silence filled the air. Well, except for the sounds of birds singing things about being happy it was summer, and bees buzzing around, and the low drone of someone mowing a lawn. I waited to see if Aisling would see what had struck me as odd.

"Why would Asmodeus want to curse the green dragons? Or is it all the dragonkin he intends to harm? Holy merde on rye, he'd have to be insane to do that. That's basically a war on dragons."

"Kinda makes you wonder, huh?" I asked, scratching a spot on my left armpit.

"It makes me do a lot more than that," she said softly. "I wonder if that's what happened to the red sept. I'm going to have to tell Drake, and he's likely to go bonkers. Oh, lord, the twins! We'll have to get them to somewhere safe … Did your friend say what form this curse would take? Or when Asmodeus was going to cast it? Or even why? We've done nothing to Abaddon! We've been too busy coping with Dr. Kostich, and Thala, and Baltic and Ysolde dying left, right, and center."

"Do you think I'd keep something important like that from you if I knew what and when Asmo was going to hit you guys with a curse?" I shook my head to myself. "Man, Ash, it's like time away from me has made you a stranger."

"You didn't tell me about the demons or the curse," she said in a mean voice.

"That's 'cause I don't know for certain there is one. Or will be one. Mehet didn't come right out and say anything about the As-man going after dragonkin. I just thought it was a bit odd he should mention it to me."

"Come home," Aisling said after another minute's silence.

"We are. I told you I'd be home by dinnertime."

"No, now. I need you now. Drake is gone for the day, and if I am going into Abaddon, I'm going to have you at my side."

"What? You're doing what?" I swear little ice cubes started floating in my veins.

Amelie emerged from the cottage, her eyes worried. "Aisling? Did I hear you say you were going to Abaddon? Surely that is not safe, is it?"

"It's a hell of a lot safer than sitting around waiting for Drake to explode worrying over something that may or may not happen. Effrijim, I summon thee."

"Byeeeeeeeeeeeeeeeee," I started to say to Amelie, but before I could finish, I thumped onto the carpet in Drake's study. "Heya, chicky," I said, giving Aisling a friendly snuffle and rub of my head. Despite all the crapola we've been through together, she's still my bestie. My noncanine bestie. "Miss me?"

"Of course I did." She leaned down and gave me a big hug and a quick fondle to the ears. "But we only have an hour before the twins are up, and I don't intend on wasting time. Let's go do a little snooping in the realm of the big bad. Effrijim, I command thee to take me to Abaddon. Somewhere safe and out of the way, where no one will see us."

I sighed again. What started out as a really good day looked like it was going to end up in the latrine.

* * *

"Right. We have to get this done quickly," Aisling said, growling slightly when her phone chirped at her.

She had tucked it away, and now muttered rude things as she dug it out of a pocket before looking at the latest text. "Drake keeps sending me texts, and he's going to suspect something is up if I don't answer him soon."

"Voice to text, babe," I said helpfully, because that's what I do. "Just turn that on and the next time he sends you a text, you can answer it without having to fight your way-too-tight jeans to get the phone out."

"My jeans are not too tight," she said with a sniff. "They're supposed to look like this. It's called fashion."

"I never heard of a fashion called 'your hips have gotten so big that you can't slip your hand in your pocket without grunting,' but whatever floats your boat." I marched down the hallway of Asmodeus's silver palace, keeping an eye out for any demons who might want to jump us.

The hallway was oddly quiet.

"That's actually not a bad idea," Aisling said, pulling her phone out again with some difficulty. "Although I dispute the comment about being broad in the beam. Right, turning on the voice-text ability." She tucked the phone into her bra, and after sketching a couple of wards on herself and me, we proceeded.

"So, where are we going?" I asked, pausing to peek around an intersection of the hallway.

"I don't know," she said with a little sniff. "You're the one who's supposed to know your way around the demon lords' palaces. Where would we find this Mehet friend of yours?"

"Dunno," I said, shrugging. "He didn't tell me where he was. He just wanted a reference to help him find a better demon lord."

"Well, great!" Aisling said with a slap of her hands on her legs. "I thought you'd know. OK. Let's think. We need to find someone here to tell us about the plan to curse the dragons. Someone low on the ladder. Can you nose a demon out who we could intimidate?"

"I could—" I started to say, but Aisling's phone made a beeping noise, and then a mechanical voice emerged from her boob as the phone converted a text to an audible form.

"From Drake. Where are you? Why are you not answering your phone?"

"Crapbeans!" Aisling said, jumping when the voice started. "Uh … Ohai! Um. Where are you? Er … end message."

The phone pinged, indicating it sent her message.

I cocked an eyebrow. She made shooing gestures, so after a few seconds' thought, I turned left and went down a flight of stairs. We'd started in what looked like a laundry area, and I figured we'd have better luck finding a low-level demon in the basement, where all good demon lords kept their administrative lackeys.

"From Drake. At home, where I expected to find you. Suzanne said you were upset about something, and summoned Jim. What has it done now?"

"Hey!" I said, glaring over my shoulder at Ash.

She made a face, then cleared her throat and answered in an unnaturally bright voice, "Nothing! Well, other than evidently be so nice that Amelie kissed it on its head, but that's a good thing. So! You came home early! That's nice."

"End message," I told her.

"Oh, yeah." She cleared her throat again and added, "End message."

I rolled my eyes, and snuffled at a door but didn't smell anyone inside. I moved on down to the next one, pausing at a blob on the floor.

"From Drake. Kincsem, you have not answered my question. Why do I have the horrible feeling you are trying to be bright and cheery and distracting?"

Aisling muttered something rude under her breath. "I'm always bright and cheery and distracting. Jim, get away from that. You don't know what sort of scat that is, and I don't want you picking up some weirdo disease because you had to snuffle demonic-being poop."

"Oh, man," I said, shaking my head.

"What?" She frowned at the blob on the ground. "Is it something bad?"

"It isn't, but your grasp on technology is," I said, walking around the imp poop to the next door.

"From Drake. Aisling. Where. Are. You. And why are you letting Jim get near any sort of excrement?"

"Crapballs," Aisling said, looking first appalled, then mean as … well, a demon lord. She stomped after me, her fingers twitching like she wanted to cast some pretty wicked wards. "I thought I told it to end the message. Er … Jim and I are on a little adventure. Just a little one. So little it's downright wee."

"Yeah, if you could call skulking around Asmo's halls wee."

Aisling had pulled her phone out of her bra, and was frantically tapping at it. "Jim! Stop talking so loud or my voice-to-text will hear you."

"From Drake. You're in Abaddon? Aisling! I forbid this!"

She glared at me at that point, just thinned her lips and outright glared at me, like it was my fault she was so inept with the latest phone technology. She even shook the phone at me when she answered, "Dammit, Jim! I told you to stop talking so loud! Now he heard you."

"Ow! Stop pinching me! Demon abuse!" I yelped when she gave my shoulder a little pinch.

"Oh, stop being such a big baby. All I pinched was fur. OK, let me try to fix this. Message to Drake. Sweetie, it's not like it sounds. We're just here following up on a rumor that Jim heard, and we'll be back shortly. Jim had a chat with one of Asmodeus's minions, and it seems like something big is up."

I licked the rumpled fur on my shoulder that she'd abused, and nosed open a door, but like the other rooms down in Asmo's offices, this one was empty of everyone, demons included.

"From Drake. I demand that you return immediately."

I snickered when I turned around and came out of the room. Aisling was still tapping wildly on her phone, even shaking it at one point. "What's so damned funny?" she asked in a whisper.

"Even the phone's default text-to-voice sounds pissed," I answered.

She glared again, and I backed up just in case she was going to try to pinch me again. She took a deep breath and made a horrible noise in the back of her throat that I realized was meant to mimic static before she said, "Sorry, phone connection is cutting out. Can't hear you. Er ... read you. We'll be back in a few minutes. Kiss kiss. End ... uh ... call. Whew. He was in a mood, wasn't he? Now, are you sure there's no one around? We can try looking upstairs, but I wouldn't want to run into any of Asmodeus's important servants. I'd never hear the end of it from Mr. Bossy if we ended up fighting a wrath demon."

"The correct phrase, which I just got done telling you, is End Message," I said just as her phone pinged again. "Also, I think you've got the auto-voice setting on."

"GAH!" she bellowed, and banged the phone against the wall a couple of times.

"From Drake. You're not going to hear the end of this for a very long time, Aisling."

She grabbed me by the collar and started dragging me back the way we came. "*Merde! Merde, merde, merde!* How the hell do you turn off the voice-to-text thing on this phone? It's stuck wide open blathering everything I say to Drake. Dammit, it's still doing it! Drake! Ignore anything you see from me! It's all a phone glitch."

"Hey," I said, putting on the brakes at a dark hallway that led off the main floor. "There's someone in there."

"In where? The men's room? I had no idea that Asmodeus had bathrooms separated by gender. I suppose ... no, never mind, it's not important now. Here's the plan: you go in and take a look-see, and tell me if it's a wrath demon or a little guy like you. If it's the latter, I'll come deal with it. If it's the former, run like hell."

"Abaddon," I corrected her, then shook myself and gave her a look that told her I didn't appreciate being referred to as a little guy.

"Hurry up," Aisling said, stuffing her phone back into her bra.

I did as she asked, and found nothing in the bathroom but a jumpy negret. It bared its sharp teeth and clacked them together at me a couple of times while it was washing its hands. "Dude," I told it, backing out of the bathroom. "No need to get your knickers in a twist. I'm outta here."

Aisling peered over my shoulder as I exited, making a face when she saw the negret. It looked offended to see her, and leaped forward to slam the door in her face.

"Well, that was a big waste of time," she said, heading toward the stairs, and the laundry room from which we'd entered Abaddon. "And all for nothing. We didn't find out one single thing, and I'm going to have enough trouble trying to calm down Drake after my phone insisted on telling him every little thing."

"From Drake," emerged from her left breast. "You don't know the half of it."

My dear Friia,

I refuse to argue with you regarding what you are calling my attempt to drive you insane. If you are such, it is surely due to your husband, and not me telling you about the trials of my children.

About which, I need not remind you, you insist on the latest news.

At this time, there is little to announce, other than my son Baltic's mate has given him a son of his own blood. I cannot help but be reminded of Baltic when he was a babe. His mother claimed he was nothing but good, but I seemed to recall many nights wherein I was obliged to walk the halls of the castle with him in my arms, in an attempt to soothe his colic.

He was always fractious, a trait that I am resigned to him passing on to his child. I am also resigned to making a visit to Baltic in order to make clear what so far the kin have missed.

I hope this message qualifies as suitably "chatty" per your demands.

Your devoted brother,
First Dragon

FOUR

ANDUIN MEETS THE FIRST DRAGON

"Mate, I insist you stop that."

I took a deep breath, gasped at the pain that cut through my irritation, and, after a few seconds spent trying to regain my ability to breathe, straightened up and glared at the love of my life. "I may not remember Brom being born, but I am fairly certain that stomping around forbidding a woman in labor from doing anything she wants to do is not smart. Or even reasonable. No, thank you, Kawaa, that one was bearable. It actually feels better to move than to sit on the birthing chair."

"Sitting is good," Baltic said in his usual bossy tone, the one that normally amuses me because I love the arrogance that is as natural to him as the breath I couldn't seem to take. "You should sit. Or lie down. Don't women having babes lie down? You will lie down."

"Your body knows what is best for it," Kawaa told me, shooting a glare over my head to where Baltic held my arm. Like him, she helped me move around the bedroom, pacing back and forth in front of a fireplace that, although not big enough to roast an ox, could have handled a pig with ease. "If you wish to walk, then we will walk."

"*Chérie*," Baltic said, his voice switching smoothly from argumentative to persuasive, "I know that you wish to rail at me due to the labor pains. I would take them from you if I could. But I would have you and the babe both get through this trial safely. The bed is comfortable. It has the linens you requested. There are many pillows."

I paused, grunting as my insides felt like they were clasped in an iron vise, one attempting to squeeze everything out of an opening that was surely too small for this. Kawaa murmured softly as I panted through the sharp edge of pain, turning to glare at the man who had put me in this position to begin with, but then I saw his eyes.

His haunted eyes, filled now with mingled love, worry, and guilt. And although it did little to ease the labor pains, my heart warmed with the fact that he, too, was suffering. I knew he was remembering the time when, so many centuries ago, we had a child who did not survive past a few hours. Baltic obviously feared that sorrow would be repeated.

"Nothing is going to happen to me," I said, tipping my head toward him until he bent to brush his lips against mine. "Or to our baby. Something might happen to you if you continue to tell me how to give birth, but only if you don't start listening to Kawaa. Oh hell, here comes another one."

Baltic didn't wait; as I doubled over, he lifted me and carried me over to the birthing chair that Kawaa had made ready.

"Keep breathing, Ysolde," Kawaa said as she dropped down to examine my nether parts. Baltic bent over to eyeball them, as well. "Ah, yes, I see things are progressing rather faster than we expected."

"What's that?" Baltic asked, pointing. "Is that supposed to be there?"

Kawaa shot him a look of disbelief before returning her attention to the action zone. "That is the head of your child. Now, please, get out of the light. If you want to make yourself useful, help brace Ysolde when the next contraction comes."

A light tap sounded at the door before it opened and Pavel stuck his head in, saying in a hushed voice, "How is it going?"

"My son's head is showing," Baltic said, and leaned down to ask me, "*Chérie*, you permit?"

I stopped panting, and looked over to the door, my brain telling me I should be outraged that Baltic would even consider allowing someone into the room while I was giving birth, but at that moment, I didn't care if an entire platoon marched through. I just wanted the baby out.

"I honestly don't give a damn," I said, the last word rising on a slight scream as another wave of pain rippled through me.

"You may enter," Baltic said grandly after the contraction, gesturing toward where my feet were now propped up, the position oddly comfortable. He had done as Kawaa said, gently helping me when I wanted to push.

Pavel's eyes widened, but he toddled into the room, followed by a tall man with a delightful Welsh accent.

"Is the baby coming, then?" Holland asked, also using the hushed tone that Pavel had adopted ever since my water broke some four hours earlier. Both men glanced at the action zone, then hurried around to a spot where it would be out of sight. "Oooh, was that the head? I'm amazed that it fits ... er ... that it can pass out ... erm ..."

I had the worst urge to burst into hysterical laughter at the fact that Holland and Pavel were now taking turns patting my shoulder, but I was too busy working my way through another contraction to do anything but scream.

"You are doing most excellently, *chérie*. You will give me another strong son, and both of you will be healthy and happy," Baltic said softly in my ear, pushing a clump of hair off my damp face.

His words were as cocky as ever, but I heard the thread of desperation hidden in them.

"I would love to reassure you—ratsbane and maggots!—but I'm busy at the moment trying not to scream down Dauva."

"This really is fascinating," Holland said to Pavel, the latter of whom was alternating his glances between Baltic, me, and a wet rag that he gently used on my sweaty face whenever I collapsed back. "Perhaps someday we should look into a surrogate. My twin sister, for instance—"

"Someday," Pavel agreed, watching me worriedly when I gave in and had a good scream at the sensation of my body being torn in two.

"Is it over yet?" The door opened again, this time revealing the form of Brom, followed immediately by Nico, the green dragon who was his tutor. "You saved the placenta, didn't you? You said I could look at it if I got through a unit of human biology, which wasn't great, although I think it is kind of cool that you grew a whole new organ just for the baby. Ew. There are all sorts of juices coming out."

I stopped screaming and glared at my son. "I agreed to let you watch the birth only because you expressed an interest in becoming a doctor. I am giving birth, Brom. There are fluids and blood and sometimes other things during a birth. You know all of that because we watched the childbirth video together."

"I will have him leave if you wish for some privacy—" Baltic murmured in my ear.

I did laugh then. The idea of privacy was long gone, but despite the intimate circumstances, I was oddly comforted by being surrounded by those I loved. "No, it's fine, so long as he wants to stay," I answered.

Brom wrinkled his nose in response, but he wasn't so disgusted that it stopped him from traipsing into the room, Nico hot on his heels. Nico averted his gaze and went to fetch more fresh water from the bathroom, but Brom, who I had high hopes would one day shift his love for all things animal to more human species, squinted at my nether parts and said, "Wow. Your vulva looks really angry. Is it supposed to be that way?"

"I am not angry, I'm in childbirth!" I said loudly.

"There is nothing wrong with your mother's genitals," Baltic said in the "instructive father" tone he had lately adopted around Brom. I didn't know if he was practicing for the baby, or had finally decided that Brom, although a superior child in all senses of the word, was starting to mimic Baltic's disregard of the opinions of others unless they allied with his own. He settled me against the back of the chair when I dropped back, exhausted from the contraction, but feeling another starting to ramp up, and leaned down to nod at my crotch. "As you can see, your brother's head is emerging."

"Crowning, it's called," Nico said as he reentered the room with a fresh bowl of water, which Holland took and dipped a rag into. "We saw that in the reproduction video, didn't we, Brom? Do you remember what the surgical incisions that Kawaa will have made are called?"

"I can't believe you're having a pop quiz now," I said to Nico, who was now engaged in tidying up some towels and small receiving blankets.

"Episiology?" Brom asked, frowning when my body decided that it was done fooling around, and it was time for the baby to be born.

"Episiotomy is the actual term—oh my. It's a baby!"

"Yuck," Brom said, frowning as he watched Kawaa deftly catch the baby. "It's all bloody. Is it supp—"

"Yes! It's supposed to look like that," I almost snapped, wondering if I should go insane now, or wait until later when everyone left, and Kawaa had sewn up my mangled remains. Heat burned through me, an odd mingling of pain, endorphins, and a sudden rush of overwhelming love as Kawaa laid the baby in my arms.

"You have a son, Ysolde," she said, a quiet joy glowing in her eyes. She even went so far as to include Baltic in her smile.

Baltic had frozen when the baby was birthed, his eyes dark and unreadable as he watched me gently wipe the infant clean. I realized after a few moments that he wasn't even breathing.

"Baltic, breathe," I said, half laughing and half crying. I was both exhausted and exhilarated. I felt like I could simultaneously sleep for a year straight and climb Mount Everest. "The baby is fine. I'm fine. Nothing has gone wrong."

"So that's an umbilical cord," Brom said thoughtfully. "It's not the color I expected. Whoa. That's gucky. And some of the baby juice splashed on Baltic."

"A boy!" Holland said, while Pavel congratulated us both, moving away when Kawaa dealt with the afterbirth. At that point, I didn't care—I was too busy marveling at the newest light dragon, feeling both protective and so much in love with him that I knew I would never want to be parted.

* * *

Three months later, I rolled over and nudged the man beside me with my toes. "Baltic, Anduin is awake. It's your turn to change him."

"I am a wyvern," he mumbled into his pillow. "It is beneath me to—ow! Mate!"

I giggled even as I gave up trying to go back to sleep, turning on the bedside light and piling pillows up behind me. "Your butt is just too delectable to keep from touching."

"Touching is fine. Touching is encouraged. I like touching. Pinching is another matter altogether," he grumbled, but, regardless, got out of bed and marched buck naked out of the room. I listened via the baby monitor to the sound of him continuing to mutter when he went into the baby's room.

"—has no respect for who or what I am. A wyvern does not tend babes! Goddesses above, what is this foulness that you have made? Ah, you think it's funny, do you! No, do not—gah! All over my chest. At least I know your bladder muscles are strong. However, now I shall have to bathe before I can return to my bed. I will have words to say to you when you are grown and can understand them, do not doubt that. There. You are clean. Are you hungry? Your mother is awaiting you now that you no longer smell like you've been dipped in the privy. Mind you do not piss on her, too. She dislikes that sort of thing."

I stifled my smile and had an innocent expression firmly in place by the time Baltic brought the baby in to me, giving the latter a dark look before he stalked off to the bathroom to wash off the baby pee.

"Don't you pay his lectures any mind," I told the baby, getting us both comfortable for a feeding. "He secretly loves taking care of you. I know this because he's made several pointed references to the fact that I had your brother before I knew Baltic was alive, but that's neither here nor there."

"He has a right to be annoyed," a deep, sonorous voice rolled slowly out of the shadows in the corner of the room.

I gasped in surprise, jerking up the sheet to cover my bare breast. "What the—oh, it's you."

The man who strolled into the puddle of light cast by the bedside lamp looked human, but he wasn't. He wasn't even a man, not really. There was a distinct sense of other about him that I suspected was *de rigueur* to all demigods.

The First Dragon paused next to me, his eyes as bright as the moon as he gazed at Anduin, happily waving his little fists while he nursed. "I visit all new dragons, child of light. All please me, but this one ..."

"Is particularly marvelous?" I said, smiling down at the baby. He watched me with the same dark-eyed intensity that I had seen so often in his father. "I agree with you about that. Did you want to say hello to your grandson?"

Anduin had released my nipple to consider the newcomer, and I deftly propped him up, gave my boob a quick wipe, and pulled the sheet up a little higher so that I wasn't exposing myself to the ancestor of all dragons who were, and who ever would be.

The First Dragon pursed his lips. Anduin, watching his grandfather, squinted in concentration for a moment, then made a rude noise.

"Would you like to hold him?" Ever one to believe the dragons, particularly the males, needed to come down off their medieval attitudes, I draped over the First Dragon's chest the small blanket that I used when nursing, and, before he could object, thrust Anduin into his hands. "No, you cradle him this way—you need to support—yes, just like that."

Although he looked a bit startled, the First Dragon gazed down at the newest member of his many descendants, and almost smiled. "It has been many centuries since I have held a babe."

"Just be aware that he has the art of projectile spitting up down pat," I said, making myself presentable in a soft, fuzzy bathrobe. "Don't hold him by his armpits or you'll end up with a face full of barf. There you are. Look who popped in to see us."

Baltic, emerging from the bathroom rubbing his wet hair with a towel, paused at the sight of the First Dragon. He assumed a dramatic pose, and narrowed his eyes at his father. "I expected he'd show up sooner or later. He always does."

"Do you know," the First Dragon said to Anduin, who had grabbed the finger the First Dragon had used to trace down his chubby cheek, "your sire and dam are most intelligent normally, but there are times when they forget who I am."

"We haven't forgotten," I said, sitting on the edge of the bed, watching as Baltic stalked naked over to his father, obviously wanting to snatch the baby away, but at the same time no doubt feeling—like me—that it was good for the First Dragon to have a little time with our baby.

"We couldn't if we wanted to. What is it you want this time? You didn't come just to see Anduin. You did that when he was barely a month old."

"He did?" I glanced at Baltic in surprise. "Why didn't you tell me?"

"It wasn't important. He visits all the babes, ours included. But for him to be here uninvited and unwanted means he's either trying to convince Brom to become a dragon or he wants something."

The First Dragon and Baltic had a complicated relationship, one where Baltic, a most favored child, was allowed to speak in a manner that would be impossible in other dragons, but there was a limit even for him, and judging by the way the First Dragon's eyes shifted from silver to gold, I figured my love had just hit that limit.

Without a word, the First Dragon handed Anduin back to me, then stood still and looked at Baltic.

I sat watching, prepared to go to Baltic's defense if he needed me, but also knowing there were some issues to be worked out between the two of them. I rocked Anduin, who was starting to get sleepy and was sucking on a couple of his chubby fingers as he sagged against me.

Baltic had never in his life backed down from a battle, but after a few minutes of glowering at his father, he finally made a disgusted noise and an abrupt gesture of capitulation. "Fine! I apologize for the 'uninvited and unwanted' comments, but if I were to show up in your bedchamber in the middle of the night, you would be less than polite to me, too."

The First Dragon thought about that for a few seconds, then gave a little nod. "I would. I am here, as you objectionably, but rightly, surmised, because of a purpose most grave." His gaze shifted to me, where I was now humming softly to Anduin. "There is much strife coming for the dragonkin. I would have you warn the other wyverns, so that they might protect their septs as best they can."

"Strife?" I asked before Baltic could. "What sort of strife?" A spurt of fear had me clutching Anduin tightly to my chest, making the baby protest sleepily. "Something dangerous for the children?"

"No. At least ..." For the first time, the First Dragon seemed to falter. "I do not believe the young are at any greater risk than the rest of the kin. My warning is for the wyverns to ensure their septs are contained and protected."

"What risk do you speak of?" Baltic asked, moving over to my side in a gesture of protection. "Who could pose a threat to the dragonkin?"

The First Dragon was silent for what seemed like minutes, but I knew must be only a few seconds. "One who once was, but is no more," he finally answered.

Before either Baltic or I could ask another question, the First Dragon met Baltic's gaze, then was gone in a little flash of light motes that sparkled in the air for a second.

"What on earth does that mean?" I asked Baltic.

He frowned, shaking his head as he sat down next to me on the bed, one arm going around my shoulders, pulling Anduin and me close. "I do not know. But I think our trip to England next week will be postponed."

I opened my mouth to protest, but the cold chill of fear brought the image to my mind of Brom and Anduin. There was no way I'd risk our children simply for the joy of returning to the home that Baltic had built for me so many centuries before. "What are you going to do?" I asked, instead.

He sat silent for a few minutes, then heaved a dramatically martyred sigh. "Do as the First Dragon wants, and warn the weyr. I wouldn't be surprised if it was all part of his plot to involve us with the other septs, just because he knows that annoys me. Is he asleep? I will take him back if you are done."

Absently, I admired Baltic's derriere as he strode out of the room with a limp Anduin. What threat could be so great that it forced Baltic into action?

A chill rippled up my spine as I rubbed my arms, suddenly cold despite the warm bathrobe.

My dear Friia,

I do not have the cellular device you mentioned; thus I have no pictures of the newest of my kin for you to enjoy. He does not resemble me particularly; he looked much like any other babe—round of cheek, and occasionally foul of odor, although I must say that I noticed he also possessed obvious intelligence and a superior manner. I have no doubt he will take after his sire and dam.

The threat to the babe Anduin and my other children has, unfortunately, grown. I have decided to speak with the Sovereign in order to provide what aid I can. I have no doubt the Sovereign can help without going too far.

Your devoted brother,
First Dragon

FIVE

WASHING A DEMON LORD OUT OF MAY'S HAIR ISN'T AS EASY AS SHE HOPED IT WOULD BE

"Sugar! I'm thrilled to little tiny bits to see that you are as adorable as ever, although a bit ... well, as we used to say in the Carrie Fay Academy of Beauty and Perky Bosoms, you're spread out like a cold supper on a hot summer night."

I froze in the act of placing some books into a packing case, closed my eyes for a second, and sent up a prayer to any deity that cared to listen. Please don't be Sally, please don't be Sally ...

"And just look who I found on your doorstep!"

"My sweet May!" a male voice said with an oily overtone that made the skin on my back crawl. Slowly, still clutching the books, I turned around to face the two people standing in the doorway of Gabriel's London house.

"Agathos daimon," I swore under my breath, habit forcing me to don a blank expression. All the long decades I had been bound to Magoth had taught me that any sign of emotions could be used against me, but even as I realized I was giving in to old habits, I relaxed. Magoth's wings had been clipped—so to speak—and I had nothing to fear from him. Not anymore. "Hello, Sally. Magoth. What brings you here to blight our doorstep?"

"Now, sugar, you know you don't mean that," Sally said with a smile that showed way too many teeth as she bustled into the room, tugging Magoth in with her. "Especially since we've come on such a mission of mercy."

"You may be here for that reason—I'm here for the wealth and power that I expect to be rained down upon me for my many and varied services," Magoth answered, stopping next to me and attempting to leer down the front of my shirt.

I clutched the books tighter to my chest, and gave him a look that would wither the testicles on any other man. "What services? What mercy? Wait—if it's going to take long to explain, don't bother telling me. I've just got this room left to pack, then I'm off to Australia."

"All alone?" Magoth made a show of peering around the room, then plucked the books from my hands and tossed them aside, trailing a cold finger across my collarbone. I slapped his hand away immediately, shivering again in response to the chill inherent to him. "What happened to your scaly boyfriend? Don't tell me he dumped you already?"

Sally giggled.

"Sally!" I said, outraged.

"What?" she asked in a syrupy drawl that always set my teeth on edge. "Oh, don't give me that look. A girl has to have a little harmless fun once in a while."

"Harmless fun it may be, but you are the Sovereign, and that means you're supposed to be on the side of right and niceness and all that." I gave a sniff and picked up the books, placing them into the packing crate before slamming the lid down on it.

"One-half of the Sovereign, dumpling, and as for the rest ... whoever told you that crock of cow cobbler?" she asked with a laugh. "My better half? Pfft. Don't listen to Terrin. He's always telling me we shouldn't get involved with mortals and people in the Otherworld, but then he goes right ahead and does that very thing. It's in his nature, just as a little teasing is in mine. And speaking of licking manly chests, where is your deliciously handsome dragon? Don't tell me Magoth is right and he's left you all on your ownsome?"

"Sweet, sweet May," Magoth said, his fingers on my chin in order to tip my head back. "The passage of time has done much to lessen my anger at your betrayal of me. Not that I would grant you the title of consort again, but the word 'plaything' has a nice ring to it, don't you think?"

I slapped his hand again, stepped back, and, taking a deep breath, bellowed one word: "Gabriel!"

"Oh, goody, he is here." Sally, clad in a cherry-red power suit, stepped over yet another box and made a show of dusting off a settee before seating herself on it. "I find that there's just nothing that brightens up a gloomy morning quite like a handsome shape-shifter, unless, of course, it's a little light bondage play."

"Bondage?" Magoth, who had pouted when I gave him a shove in order to heft the packing crate over to a stack next to the door, looked much more cheerful. "By light, do you mean level of intensity, or well-lit properties? I do hope it's the latter, since filming a truly detailed bondage session is a waste of time if you don't have adequate lighting to highlight every exquisite moment of the lash falling on tender, quivering flesh."

My shoulders sagged. "Why are you here?" I asked, figuring it would be faster in the end to let them explain rather than to try to ignore their unwanted presence. "Specifically, why are you together? I thought you were in California, Magoth. What happened to your film studio?"

He shrugged, and removed his shirt. Magoth disliked being clothed, and was never happier than when he could show off the tattooed curse on his penis. "My seneschal is dealing with the studio crisis—you remember him? He used to be one of my demons, but Sally kicked him out of Abaddon when she was one of the princes."

"Briefly one of the princes," Sally corrected. "The briefly part is important, since technically, being part of the Sovereign means I can't also rule in Abaddon, but you know, only people with tiny minds focus on minutiae like that. May, dumpling, are you wearing that outfit just for housework, or do you go out in public like that? I ask as a friend, as someone who cherishes you for the unique style that is all your own."

"There is nothing wrong with my clothes," I answered without even looking down at myself. Since I was wearing a pair of black leggings, a simple white shirt, and a leather vest that hid a couple of daggers, I knew my appearance was untoward. "And yes, I can see where being the leader of heaven and hell at the same time is a breach of etiquette, but that isn't why you're here. Asmodeus is in charge of Abaddon now. Which brings me around, yet again, to why you are here."

"Why is who—ah." Gabriel appeared at the door, all six feet two of delicious dragon in man form, his hair shorter now that he'd chopped off his dreadlocks. But his eyes, his mercurial silver eyes, were just as bright as they ever were, filling me with a heat that I knew would never fade. "I see we have visitors. Magoth, I would appreciate it if you would put, at the very least, your trousers back on; we've all seen your cursed cock far too many times. Sally, it is a pleasure to have you grace our abode."

Gabriel was the master of bowing, making the anachronistic gesture seem elegant and perfectly suited to the situation, and the one he executed now was charming enough that a pink glow of pleasure lit Sally's cheeks.

"I'm so happy to see you again … and darling May, of course." Sally patted the cushion next to her, an invitation I'm sorry to say Gabriel took as he seated himself beside her. "And I'm pleased as three types of tutti-frutti punch to know you have not let May's lax ways drive you from her side. It says much about your character that you would stick by her regardless of her inattention to her outer self. But then, you are a very charming man."

"Sally!" I said again, reaching into my vest to pull out one of my daggers, which I examined with studied nonchalance. "If you do not take your hand off of Gabriel's thigh in the next two seconds, I will see to it that you do not have a hand to bother with—"

"Now you see," she said in a confidential tone to Gabriel, although I noticed she did remove her hand from where it had been stroking his leg. "This is why I have always said May was meant to be dear Magoth's consort. Have you ever heard such threats against one who is known for her benevolence and general goodwill toward all?"

Gabriel's lips twitched, but he said simply, "May has little patience for foolishness, as do I. To what do we owe the pleasure of your presence? And that of Magoth."

"Fame, fortune, and fornication are the reasons I'm here," the latter replied, thankfully now having put his pants on again. He had claimed the sofa across the room, and was lying on it in a dramatic pose that I knew he'd practiced to express both raw sexual attraction and languid grace. "All of which I expect you to provide me for my services rendered."

"He keeps saying that," I said, and, with nowhere else to sit since most of the furniture had been put into storage, parked myself sideways across Gabriel's lap. "And before you ask, no, I did not promise him fornication, or anything else, for that matter."

Gabriel's arm went around me, giving me a gentle squeeze, but his eyes danced with amusement. "What service do you feel we need from you?" he asked Magoth.

"Ask her," Magoth said, waving a hand toward Sally. "I'm too exhausted from the flight from California to do more than recover my strength. Do you have any house slaves? I could use a massage."

"Gabriel, Tipene would like to know if you want him to close up the lair, or if there are more things you wish to pull from it—" The woman who appeared at the door paused, her silver gaze flicking from where I sat on Gabriel, to Sally, then over to Magoth. Her eyes narrowed on him before she turned back to face us, obviously asking a silent question.

"We didn't invite them. They showed up of their own accord, claiming they have something we need," I told Maata, one of Gabriel's two elite guards. She, like Gabriel and Tipene, was of indigenous Australian ethnicity, and was one of the few people I trusted as much as the man who held my heart.

Magoth propped himself up on an elbow and cocked an eyebrow at me before eyeing Maata. "I have many ways to fulfill needs, both base and primal. Your dragon servant there—does she shift into bestial form often? Is her tail as powerful as yours, sweet May?"

"Oh, for the love of—no, don't answer him, Maata. He'll only enjoy that," I said, ignoring Gabriel's chuckle that brushed the side of my neck. "Sally, as the sanest member of your little duo, would you please tell us why you are blighting us with Magoth?"

"Blight!" Magoth said in an outraged tone, then added thoughtfully, "Now, I haven't inflicted a good blight in, oh, centuries. Hmm. I wonder what I could work up with the little power you ensured I was left with?"

"Tell Tipene to close the lair," Gabriel told Maata, tapping me on the hip. I scooted off him while he stood up, speaking with her quietly for a moment before she left the room.

"Well, you're going to need someone to go with you to Abaddon, and who better to help you find your way around than Magoth?" Sally said, examining one fingernail.

"Abaddon?" Gabriel and I both said at the same time. I moved over to lean against him, drawing both comfort and strength from the warmth of his body.

"Why would May want to go to Abaddon?" he asked.

"To find out what this curse is all about, of course," Sally said, tsking and pulling from a pocket an emery board. "Since your Guardian friend didn't get any information when she was there."

"Aisling went to Abaddon?" I asked, surprised. "Why?"

"To learn more about the curse," Sally answered, waving the emery board in a vague gesture.

I looked at Gabriel. He looked back at me. We both turned to look at Sally. "What curse?" Gabriel asked.

"The one that's being set upon dragons." Surprise was writ on her face. "You can't say you don't know about that! It's all over the Otherworld."

"Another curse?" I said, feeling a familiar sense of despair well up inside of me. "The silver dragons just got rid of one. Why are we being cursed now?"

"And by whom?" Gabriel asked, his brows pulling together in a frown. I could feel anger within him, anger that whipped up his dragon fire. Since Gabriel normally had extremely good control of his fire, I was more than a little surprised at the intensity of it.

"That's what you're going to Abaddon to find out, sugar," Sally said, her expression all innocence.

I didn't trust that expression any more than I trusted Magoth.

"We don't know what you are talking about," Gabriel said, smoothly courteous as ever. He had great respect for Sally, given who she was, but I felt he had misplaced his judgment when it came to her. She was as slippery as an eel when she wanted to be. "Would you explain?"

She made an annoyed tch, put away her emery board, and rose to strike a pose in front of the fireplace. "Really, I'm surprised that y'all should be so unaware of something that could be devastating to all the dragons, but that's neither here nor there really, is it? Rumor has it that a curse is being woven in Abaddon."

"Woven?" I asked, glancing at Gabriel. "Magoth never wove curses. He'd just send out his demons to cast them on whoever he wanted doomed."

"After suitable sacrifices of those demons who irritated me, naturally," Magoth said, once again prone on the couch, this time with an arm across his forehead in mock exhaustion. "And some who didn't irritate me, but who made lovely squishy sounds when—"

"The most powerful curses are woven, not cast, little bird," Gabriel interrupted, tossing an annoyed glance toward Magoth. "Just as the one Baltic placed upon us was woven. But I have heard of no such curse being created now. Who is your informant, Sally?"

"My better half, actually." She ran a finger along a now empty bookshelf, and made a face at the resulting dust. "Terrin, as I have mentioned, interests himself greatly in both mortals and immortals, despite knowing that such things often lead only to trouble on our part. But he is what he is, and he is seldom wrong, so when he asked me to provide May with an escort through Abaddon, naturally I thought of darling Magoth."

Magoth moved his arm enough to give her a lascivious look.

"But why do I have to go to Abaddon?" I asked, moving tighter against Gabriel. I'm no coward, but the last thing I wanted to do was spend time in the realm of demons and their princes. I'd been there, done that, and really didn't want to go back.

"You don't," Gabriel answered, his arm warm and solid around me. "There is no reason for you to put yourself at such risk."

"There is if you want to find out what form the curse will take," Sally pointed out. "Your Guardian friend failed. Evidently her dragon kicked up such a fuss about her being there that she had to leave without getting the information she sought. Thus, therefore, and all those official-sounding phrases that Terrin loves so dearly, it's up to you to succeed where she failed."

"Which is where I come in," Magoth said, suddenly sitting upright. "Now, shall we discuss my fee for my invaluable and irreplaceable services? Not only will I require enough money to pay off that pesky taxation organization in the States that insists my studio is in arrears, but also, I will require seven sacrifices—virgins, of course—along with three boons from an archimage, and sweet May's presence in my playroom."

I looked up at Gabriel. "I think we need to talk."

"Yes," he answered, his gaze flickering over to Magoth. "I believe that would be an excellent idea."

Without waiting, I shadowed, using my doppelganger abilities to slip into the shadow world, what most people called the Beyond, a plane of existence that normally held beings of magic origins such as mages and the fey. Gabriel, son of a shaman, followed me into it. In the distance, I could hear Sally exclaim, "Magoth, did you see that? They just blipped right out without saying so much as boo. I consider that quite, quite rude. One doesn't blip into the Beyond without at least an offer of sweet tea and snickerdoodles to hold us over while they are gone."

"What do you think?" I asked Gabriel softly. We couldn't be seen by Magoth and Sally, but if we spoke loudly, they might be able to hear us. "Much as I hate to believe Sally, she's never actually lied outright."

"No, she hasn't," Gabriel answered slowly, his eyes darkened somewhat by the dim light of the shadow world. "I don't understand why a demon lord would weave a curse to affect dragonkin, but assuming one is doing so, it behooves us to investigate."

"Then I'll have to go," I said, pulling out both daggers, since holding them made me feel a tiny bit better about the idea of going back to literal hell.

"Not you, no," he answered with a slow smile and matching warmth in his eyes.

"You're not planning on taking my place—" I started to say, about to make a big fuss.

"I would if it was needful, but there is an alternative to either of us traipsing through Abaddon, no doubt attracting far too much attention."

"There is? Who? It sounds like Drake had a major hissy fit over Aisling being there, so who else—" I paused in the act of casting my mind over our acquaintances, wondering who amongst them could visit Abaddon without anyone noticing, when the obvious struck me. Aisling might not be able to return to Abaddon, but that didn't mean her demon couldn't. "Oh, I see. Yes, but would Aisling let Jim do it?"

"I don't see why not. It knows its way around Abaddon better than anyone, and if we charged Magoth with protecting Jim, then it wouldn't be at risk."

I stood on tiptoe to kiss the tip of his nose. "You have such a fabulous brain. That's why I love you."

He pulled me into a fast, hard, and very hot kiss before following me back into the real world.

"—and I told her that there was nothing we could do about the timing of the renaissance, and ready or not, she'd just have to pull up her big-girl pants and do the job. Did you want me to draw blood? Oh, is this a sensitive spot? Well, as I was saying, Terrin wants a break, and of course, I have so many delicious hobbies, so it really could not be coming at a better time. Darlin', I can't possibly understand you with that ball gag in your mouth. Should I remove it? I could put it—why,

there you both are. I thought you'd gone and left us."
Sally stood above a once-again naked Magoth as he lay facedown, spread-eagle on the rug with his arms and legs bound to the two remaining pieces of furniture. She held a leather lash in one hand, and a candle in the other.

Gabriel gave a little eye roll. "Magoth, get up. If you've stained the carpet, you will pay for the cleaning."

Magoth said something that was too muffled to understand, but made a humping motion that I hoped was him trying to squirm out of his bonds, and not something much less savory.

"May—"

"On it," I told Gabriel, and, with a flick of one of my daggers, cut the nylon cord used to tie Magoth down. He rolled over, causing me to look elsewhere, since I had a feeling he was enjoying himself far too much. "Right, we've come to a decision," I told Sally while Gabriel hauled Magoth to his feet and threw his pants at him.

"Sugar, I'm waiting with breath that isn't just bated—it's a downright smorgasbord of anticipation," she said, giving me another of her toothy smiles.

"We agree that someone needs to investigate this threat of a curse," I said. "But I will not be doing the grunt work. Although Magoth's offer of his assistance will be accepted."

Gabriel gave Magoth a long look. "Naturally, we will pay you a reasonable amount for your help, but there will be no sacrifices, virgin or otherwise, nor will any of your other demands be met, especially those concerning my mate."

"You know how to take fun out of any situation," Magoth told Gabriel with a hauteur that was at odds with the fact that we'd just discovered him humping the rug while being flogged by one of the two people who ran what most mortals thought of as heaven. He added a little annoyed sniff before saying, "Since my seneschal informs me the mortals won't allow the studio to open without some sort of tithe in monetary form, then I will accept your offer of currency." He named a sum that had me sighing to myself.

Gabriel managed to beat him down to a price that I thought was outrageous, but which was evidently acceptable in both their eyes.

"But if you aren't going to Abaddon with Magoth, who is?" Sally asked.

"Aisling's demon, Jim." I pinned Magoth back with a look that warned I would have no shenanigans on his part. "And if you value your cursed penis, you'll take very good care of it."

Magoth glanced down at his fly before smirking at me. "I always do, sweet one."

"I meant Jim the demon, and you know it."

Magoth pouted a little at that, but after another ten minutes of discussing the details, we managed to shoo them on their way.

"We'll have to delay our departure for a few days," I told Gabriel as Sally and Magoth trotted down the front steps to the sidewalk below.

Sally paused on the lowest step, casting a glance back at me that was so unlike her normal bright expression, it sent chills through my veins. "Oh, it's going to take more than a few days, sugar," she warned. "The sorrow has already begun. Gather your dragonkin now, lest they, too, be swept up in the annihilation."

She was off before I could do more than gape at her in horror.

"Gabriel?" I asked without turning to look at him.

"I'll call Drake," he said, pulling out his phone.

"And I'll alert the other mates," I said, worry, and fear, and anxiety, making me feel mildly nauseous as I watched Sally and Magoth disappear around the corner. I didn't even want to think about how a demon lord's curse could affect dragonkin.

My dear Friia,

I do not understand why you persist in desiring "drama updates" on my kin. You say it is better than your favorite opera, although I fail to see what soap has to do with the theater. Thus, I can only conclude that your senses are addled from too much time with dolphins. That or Óðinn is driving you insane, which would not shock me. He is quite, quite mad, you know.

Unfortunately, I have little time to help you recover your common sense. A great tragedy is poised to claim my children, and I must do what I can to help them from all being destroyed.

Your devoted brother,
First Dragon

SIX

WYVERNS ARE MASTERS OF DISTRACTION

Jian Tin Text Messages

To: Wyverns

It turns out that news of my demise was not quite true. With Li's help, I have escaped the prison into which Chuan Ren placed me before she was killed.

Li has given me dire news about the state of my sept. I don't have all the details of what went on while I was incarcerated, but once I locate sept members and am caught up, I will be in contact.

From: Drake

Chuan Ren imprisoned you? Would it be impolitic of me to ask why? Regardless, I am glad to know you are still amongst us.

From: Gabriel

It might be impolitic, but I will admit to curiosity, as well. May and I are delighted to hear that you have been released, although I wish someone from your sept had told us of your imprisonment.

To: Wyverns

From what I've been told, only a few of my kin

knew. Chuan Ren took umbrage with my suggestion that we work with the weyr to locate and capture Fiat Blu, and since she has never been entirely balanced on the subject of Fiat, she was determined to seek revenge for his acts against her and the red dragons without assistance from anyone else. She made many claims about me that I would prefer not to dwell on, with the end result that Mak—my lieutenant—and I were imprisoned. She told no one where we were, and left us to starve. Luckily, Li survived Chuan Ren's death, and stumbled across us while gathering up her belongings.

From: Kostya

Christos! I know well what it's like to be imprisoned and tormented. As for your sept ... there is much we have to tell you, but it can wait until you speak to those red dragons who still live.

To: Wyverns

Still live? Li said that many of our sept were missing, but not that they are dead. Was it Fiat? This is most distressing. I must speak with Li and determine what happened while we were incarcerated. I will contact you when I have been given more information.

To: Wyverns

My apologies for not being in contact since I last messaged you three days ago. I regret to inform the weyr that the sept of the red dragons has been decimated. To date, Mak and I have located only two other members. The rest have been killed by demons and the monstrosities that Asmodeus has made. My heart is filled with such sorrow it has turned the world to darkness. Li is diminishing, but he did mention I should look to the dragon hunters for information.

I am leaving immediately for the West Coast of the United States, where it is reported two dragon hunters reside. Once I find one of them, I hope to have some answers about how Asmodeus has destroyed the sept of the red dragons.

From: Drake

The hearts of all in the weyr are heavy with shared sorrow at the loss of our brothers and sisters. We will be in contact as we learn new information.

DRAGONBOOK

Social Media for the Weyr

May Northcott Video Group: Wyverns and Mates

Slowly, one by one, the pictures popped up on the group video-call software. Aisling and Ysolde were the first two who appeared.

"Houston, we have a problem," I said before the ladies could do more than pop their earbuds in and adjust their respective tablets and phones. As they were doing so, a few more pictures of dragons blipped into being.

"That's putting it mildly," Aisling said, glancing to her side and saying, "No, Jim, you don't need to get your own earphones. I'll tell you what everyone says. I assume you're talking about the red demons, May? We haven't seen any more of them since Drake and Kostya dealt with the ones who attacked us."

"What is this?" Jian's image wobbled briefly as he apparently propped up his phone. His voice sounded tinny and distant, assumedly from a less-than-sterling Internet connection. "You have seen more? We have been trying to locate any other remaining members of my sept, but if you have seen more of those abominations—"

"No, I said we haven't seen any others than the ones who attacked us in the club," Aisling said in a voice filled with sympathy. "And you know we all feel awful about the destruction of your sept. If there's anything we can do beyond searching for any of your members who haven't been tainted, let us know."

There were murmurs of sympathy as more dragons logged into the video software.

Jian bowed his head in acknowledgment of the offer, although I knew that all the wyverns had been in contact with him privately to offer sympathy, advice, and help.

Aisling dabbed at her eyes with a tissue, then added, "Although I still don't understand why the ones who attacked us at the club would want a mage sword, since they can't use it. Assuming that's why they were there, and I see no other reason why they would have swarmed that location."

"Wait, what?" I asked, glancing at Gabriel, who had come into the room and sat beside me to watch the others as they logged into the video call. "What red demons? What club? Are you talking about Baltic's mage sword that Dr. Kostich took?"

"Oh lord, didn't you tell them, Drake?" Aisling asked.

Drake, who was apparently located in another room because he had his own video feed, raised his eyebrows. "I have just spoken with Gabriel, but have not had a chance to tell the others. Gabriel wishes to call a sárkány, but I suppose since we are all gathered here now, we could have a brief update of the situation. Jian, are you up to discussing the fate of your kin?"

Jian rubbed a hand over his face. His expression was drawn and obviously distressed. "No, but my desires do not matter in the face of the horror that has beset my sept. As best I understand it, more than half of the red dragons have been slaughtered outright by a large number of demons, while the rest were taken and tormented until they themselves became demonic beings. I do not understand how they could be so changed—"

"A demon lord," Aisling interrupted, then apologized. "Sorry, Jian. Go ahead."

He gestured tiredly. "You are the expert here, Aisling. Please, feel free to explain it to the others."

Aisling settled back against the couch, Jim moving over to sit next to her. "Well, as near as we can figure it, Asmodeus—for some bizarre reason that I don't think any of us understand—decided to wipe out the red sept." She hesitated a moment, glancing at Jim.

"What?" Jim asked, its eyes round with what I knew it thought of as a look of pure innocence.

"I thought perhaps you might have some insight into why Asmodeus would want to destroy the red dragons."

"I might have if we'd been able to talk to the steward, but since Drake was being Mr. Unreasonable—ack!"

A crown of fire burst into being on Jim's head, which Aisling absently patted out before saying, "Point taken. Jim and I made a little trip to Abaddon, but it was called short because Drake took issue with us being there. Where was I?"

"About to award Drake a trophy for the most distant use of fire on a demon?" Ysolde asked with a quirk of her lips.

Aisling gave a half smile. "He's very good with his fire, but that's neither here nor there."

Drake tried to look humble, but failed.

"So long story short—Jim, don't you dare say anything, or I won't put out the fire the next time you lip off to Drake—long story short, we don't know why Asmodeus decided he'd wipe out the red sept by turning the members into these weird half-dragon, half-demon hybrids, but he did, and they are really nasty customers. Although evidently many of them are now … er … gone."

"Yeah. Permanently," Jim said, drawing a paw across its throat with a horrible noise.

"Jim!" Aisling whomped it on the shoulder. "That is unfeeling and cruel to Jian, since they were his former sept members, and you can just be silent unless you have something useful to say."

"It's all right," Jian said with another little gesture that seemed to ooze despair. "Your demon speaks the truth. You both do. I don't know what the demon lord Asmodeus did to my kin, or why he picked my sept, but the results were monstrous."

"More than twenty of the red demons were killed at their attack in Paris," Kostya said, coming into view as his image popped up.

"By the rood!" Ysolde said, looking horrified. "I don't know which is more appalling—that your sept would be so devastated, or the fact that Asmodeus is going to try to destroy us all by making us demons. Baltic, are you on this chat? I can't see who is who, since half the squares are clumped up on my phone screen."

"Yes, I am here, but I would like to know why you are awake. You should be resting. You are still recovering from the birth," Baltic answered, his video square popping up briefly. His face was mostly in shadow, and I realized he was in a car.

"What are we going to do?" Ysolde asked, her eyes narrowing. "Clearly, this must be what the First Dragon was talking about."

"You've had a visit from him?" I asked, feeling a sudden warm glow in my stomach at the mention of the demigod dragon progenitor. Ysolde and I had a special connection to the First Dragon due to the dragon heart shard that we had both once borne, so I was always interested in his visits.

"Briefly, yes. He was his usual mysterious self, saying something horrible was going to happen, and for Baltic to warn the weyr, but why he couldn't just tell us that the red dragons were going to be attacked—or warn Jian himself—is beyond me," Ysolde answered.

"I don't know," I said slowly, glancing at Gabriel. "I'm not sure—"

"May and I have also had a visit recently, although not from the First Dragon," he said, and briefly explained about Sally's insistence that we investigate Abaddon to locate information about the curse.

"So on top of Asmodeus wiping out dragon septs, he's going to curse the rest of us?" Ysolde asked, her face pinched with worry. "Baltic—"

"Do not worry, mate. I will allow no harm to come to you or the children," Baltic answered immediately. "As for this supposed curse—I don't see any purpose to it. It cannot benefit Asmodeus."

"You may not think so, but something is definitely up," Aisling said, shaking her head. "And if the First Dragon is warning us—well, I guess it's understandable that Drake had a hissy fit when we came back from Abaddon and is trying to see if a château he owns in the French countryside, which he never bothered to tell me about, is secure enough for the twins while all this goes down."

Drake donned a martyred expression. "All Abaddon is evidently about to break loose, and you choose to be annoyed at the fact that I haven't given you a detailed list of all my real estate interests?"

Bastian's image popped onto the grid of faces. "What's this about Abaddon breaking loose?"

Ysolde, Aisling, and Gabriel brought him up to speed while I was mulling over something that Jian had said earlier.

Once Bastian was current with the latest details, I asked, "Who did you say you were going to see, Jian?"

"A dragon hunter," he answered, his voice as bleak as his expression.

"A what, now?" Aisling asked.

"Dragon hunter," he answered, and turned to look to the side when another dragon appeared, no doubt his friend Mak, with whom he had been imprisoned.

"What's a dragon hunter?" Aisling looked as confused as I felt. "A hunter looking for dragons, or a dragon who hunts?"

No one answered her.

She made an exasperated tch in the back of her throat. "Drake?"

"What?"

"What's a dragon hunter?"

"*Kincsem*, I am two rooms away from you. Why are you asking questions here when you could be asking me in person?"

Aisling, Ysolde, and I all made what I was sure was the same face.

"Because you guys are horrible about answering a direct question," Aisling pointed out, and Ysolde and I nodded. "You always sidestep the issue and try to distract us with something unrelated in order to avoid doling out information. A suspicious person might think you like us to be ignorant about all things dragon."

"Baltic is a master at the misdirect," Ysolde said. "You wouldn't believe how hard it is to get a straight answer out of him."

"If that is so, it is because I have a mate who drives me to distraction worrying about her. You should not be awake at this time, Ysolde. As I have repeatedly reminded you, the silver wyvern's mother told you that you need to rest, or you will get those painful leg cramps again."

Aisling winced. "Oh man, I hate those. Keep your feet up higher than your heart, Ysolde. It really helps with puffy ankles, too."

"I have been doing nothing but sitting with my feet elevated for two months, not that my ankles could be in any way described as ankle-ish," Ysolde answered with a sigh. "They are more like small watermelons attached to my feet."

"You should see mine," Aisling said with a sympathetic moue. "I'm only two months along, but I have the ankles of a woman three weeks past her due date. Dammit."

"What?" Ysolde asked, looking mildly startled at the exclamation.

Aisling pointed to the screen. "They did it again."

I gave a little cough. "I wasn't going to say anything, not suffering from pre- or postnatal issues—and I hope you're feeling better soon, Ysolde, watermelon ankles and all—but yes, you'll notice the men have all stopped talking because they don't want to answer our questions."

"That or we don't want to be drawn into discussions of what having watermelon ankles entails," Kostya said dryly.

Immediately, Baltic's square lit up. "Ysolde's ankles are not watermelons! They are delicate and perfectly formed, just as is the rest of her! Take back your slander, Konstantin Fekete, or I will be forced yet again to teach you how to speak to my mate."

Aisling, Ysolde, and I all giggled. Kostya just looked enraged, as per normal.

"I did not slander anyone, let alone Ysolde, for whom I have the greatest respect, which you well know, you deranged old man. She, herself, likened her ankles to watermelons. And if anyone is going to teach anyone else a lesson, it will be me. To you. That is, I will teach you. A lesson, that is. One that is sorely overdue."

"Oh for the love of Pete." Aisling tapped a button that made a loud horn sound in the software. "We are not doing this, gentlemen. And, Baltic, before you think about starting something with Kostya in order to distract us, just don't. We don't have time for you two and your endless pissing contest."

"Hear, hear," Gabriel said, nodding. "Let us move past Kostya's and Baltic's many respective faults and focus on what is important."

I gave him a gimlet glance that he refused to meet, although his dimples flashed.

Kostya, as I knew he would, took umbrage. "Faults! I like that! I have no faults! It's not like I cursed an entire sept. Not that you didn't deserve it, but still. I didn't do that. And I could have if I wanted to."

Next to me, Gabriel stiffened. Although my beloved was normally the most patient of men, Kostya still managed to press Gabriel's hot buttons. "You and what army?" he asked.

I couldn't help myself. I leaned to the side and kissed his cheek, saying, "Boom! Point for Team Silver."

"The black dragons were around long before that deranged maniac Constantine ripped our kin apart to make your sept," Kostya snarled with suitably dramatic flared nostrils. "So you don't get the point; it goes back to us by default."

"They're doing it again. This time by arguing," Ysolde pointed out.

Aisling made a face. "So they are. Right, end of rehashing old history. We have more than enough on our plates as is. Now, back to May's point. Er ... I've forgotten what it was."

"Well, it was going to be discussing the horrible things apparently happening in Abaddon, but before we get to that, what exactly is a dragon hunter?" I asked. "I've never heard of them before."

"Yes, good question." Ysolde nodded. "I'm curious about that, too. Baltic, do you know?"

Baltic looked almost as annoyed as Kostya. "Yes."

"And?" Ysolde asked when he offered no more than the one word.

He did a little nostril flaring of his own. "Stay where you are. Pavel and I will be home shortly, at which time I will go to the bedchamber to make sure that you are resting."

"Great." Ysolde heaved a big sigh. "Now Kostya has made Baltic cranky."

"I am not cranky," Baltic objected. "I am, however, worried about a mate who is cavalier about her health a few short months after birthing."

I gestured at the camera in the laptop. "Distraction, thy name is wyvern."

Gabriel stifled an amused snort.

Aisling, who had been nodding, said, "Yup. Jian, you have the floor. Please tell us about dragon hunters."

"Er ..." Jian looked momentarily disconcerted. "I'm not sure I should. If the other wyverns don't wish it to be discussed ..."

"Look," Ysolde interrupted. "We can do this the easy way, or we can do this the hard way. I'm up for the hard way, but I don't think any of the wyverns are going to like me asking Dr. Kostich for information about dragonkin business."

Baltic's square flashed. "You will not contact the insane archimage."

Ysolde pursed her lips. "Think you can stop me?"

"Yes, I do," he answered immediately.

Ysolde narrowed her eyes at the screen.

I gave her a thumbs-up. Gabriel rolled his eyes.

Baltic, dread wyvern though he might be, knew when he'd met his match. Immediately, he switched his attitude from domineering to suave. "*Chérie*, this argument is ridiculous. We will be home in a half hour. We will discuss the matter then. In the privacy of our bedchamber."

"Oh, don't think I don't know that tone of voice," Ysolde said with a little snort. "Even on that tiny picture, I can see you trying to distract me with your sexy, sexy self."

"It's working, isn't it?" Baltic asked with a hint of a smile.

"Yes, but only because I know you'll rub my watermelon ankles later," she answered. "Jian, spill. Yes, that's an order, and yes, I know I have no power to give you an order, but still, as the oldest established mate, and one who remembers when you were a wee red dragon, I would appreciate it if you would stop giving us the runaround and explain what a dragon hunter is."

Jian hesitated before he answered. "Dragon hunters are ... myths."

"Huh?" Aisling looked even more confused. I didn't blame her.

"Technically speaking, they do not exist," Drake explained. "They are demons, nothing more."

"That's not quite true," Gabriel said, shifting next to me. "They were part dragon to start with, or so my mother told me. Wasn't the first dragon hunter a green dragon?"

Drake looked sour. "No. He had green kin, but he was ouroboros. Beyond that, he had nothing to do with the sept or weyr."

"Do not forget that the monster stole a blue dragon and forced her to bear his vile demon spawn," Bastian added.

"Wait, so dragon hunters are demons who, what, want to off dragons?" Aisling shook her head again. "Like the guys we saw in Paris who attacked us at the club?"

No one answered.

I nudged Gabriel. "Well?" I asked him.

He refused to meet my eyes.

"Baltic?" Ysolde tried her wyvern, to no more effect than me.

Aisling tsked. "You guys can't ghost us on this, you know. For one, we know where you live. For another, with the exception of Baltic evidently being out of Dauva at the moment, you're home, and if you really want us to give you pointed looks in person, we'll do it. I, myself, have a few choice things to say to a certain wyvern about his reticence in sharing information pertinent to the woman he says makes his life worth living."

I let Gabriel have my very best pointed look. He just winked at me.

"Baltic." Ysolde narrowed her eyes at the screen. "I know full well you are still here because your icon keeps pulsing with annoyed snorting sounds. Are the dragon hunters demons, or dragons?"

It took a few seconds, but at last Baltic answered. "They are not kin."

"See?" Ysolde smiled at the screen. "That didn't hurt."

"Like hell it didn't. You wanted me to rejoin the weyr, and now you have made me say things in front of the other wyverns that will give them the ability to raise an eyebrow at me. I just want you to remember this the next time you coerce me into doing things I don't want to do," he answered, sounding as testy as usual.

Aisling gave a little laugh, and said, "You're a big strong boy, Baltic. I'm sure you'll get over a little eyebrow raising, not that I believe any of the wyverns will do that, because they know which side their respective bread is buttered. Well, the mated ones, anyway. The big question is whether they are the guys who attacked the club in Paris."

"No," Drake said after a moment's thought. "At least, they did not seem so to me. Kostya?"

Kostya looked pensive for a few moments, finally saying, "I agree. They were something else. There was no sense of dragon about them, only demon."

"OK, so dragon hunters which are not the red demon-dragon dudes that attacked us in the Paris club have been seen on the West Coast of the US, according to Jian," Aisling said. "That jibes with what Jim said about there being big doings in Abaddon, and with Asmodeus sending out demons to target dragons, although I assumed the latter were the red demony dragons we saw and beat to a pulp."

"And then there's the curse," I said, glancing at Gabriel. "Sally said that someone in Abaddon was weaving a curse to cast upon us. Obviously, that must be Asmodeús, since you seem to have confirmation of that fact."

"Weaving?" Aisling asked, her brow furrowed. "Curses can be woven?"

"Yes," all the wyverns answered at the same time.

"Sheesh," she said, glaring at the screen. "OK, I get it. But ... we're back to what curse? And why is Asmodeus—and yes, there's no other demon lord with that sort of power—why is he cursing us? What does a demon lord expect to get by cursing the dragonkin except a whole lot of pissed-off dragons?"

"Sally wanted me to go to Abaddon and sneak around to find out. That's why she brought Magoth with her," I said.

Gabriel was shaking his head even before I finished. "May will not be going to Abaddon. It is too dangerous for her. Jim, however, is another matter. Would you be willing to let it undertake such a job, Aisling?"

"Hmm." Aisling looked thoughtful, and glanced at the dog next to her. "I suppose so, assuming Jim is willing to go. I wouldn't make it if it didn't want to. Jim, you may speak."

"Fires of Abaddon," the demon said, gasping as if it had been holding its breath. "I hate it when you order me to silence. Heya, everyone. How they hangin'? Respectively, that is."

"Jim," Aisling said, her voice filled with warning.

Jim grinned at her. "Yeah, yeah, but you wouldn't want me to be rude, would you?"

"How do you feel about going to Abaddon on your own?" Aisling asked it.

"Oh, Jim wouldn't be alone—Magoth has agreed to accompany it to keep it safe," I said quickly. "And of course, if Jim doesn't want to go … well, we'd never force it. We just thought that since it knows its way around better than I do—not to mention it can change its form to fit in better than me—that it would be ideal."

Jim's eyes lit up. "So I'd be like an undercover demon? A superspy demon? Do I get a gun with a silencer?"

"No gun," Aisling said, obviously thinking over the proposition. "No silencer. I'd have to temporarily bind Jim to Magoth—otherwise he wouldn't have the ability to guard Jim from danger. It's a demon lord thing. OK, so if we have Jim and Magoth poking around Abaddon to suss out details about the curse, is there anything else we should be doing? Other than keeping our eyes peeled for any non-demon red dragons, of course."

"I would appreciate you doing so, although there are only a handful of my sept who are unaccounted for, and we fear they were killed, as well," Jian said wearily. "I am in the US now, on my way to California to track down the rumored dragon hunter."

Drake frowned. "With all due respect to Li's suggestion you speak to one, I don't see how this dragon hunter you mention can be related to the red hybrids we saw here. Is that what you are thinking?"

"That's a difficult question to answer," Jian said slowly. "I don't know if you told the others about the conversation we had when you saw the red dragon hybrids—"

"I haven't had time, no," Drake answered.

Jian nodded. "When I heard about the monsters who attacked you in Paris, I assumed Asmodeus had taken members of my sept and corrupted them. But after we found remains, and interviewed witnesses, it became clear that the demons were not born of my sept. If they were red dragons, they must have left before Chuan Ren was imprisoned in Abaddon. I had heard there was some sort of a split once Fiat claimed the sept, but as I was … incommunicado … at that time, I had no specific details."

"Chuan Ren imprisoned you other times, as well?" Aisling asked, looking askance.

Jian made an indeterminate gesture. "Her temper could be volatile, and I was the nearest at hand to it."

There were a few murmurs of agreement regarding Chuan Ren's notoriously short temper before Jian continued.

"Once I took over the sept, it became clear that some members were missing. I was told they had gone ouroboros during my earlier confinement. It is my belief—given what Drake and Kostya experienced in Paris—that the supposed red dragons they saw there were those ouroboros members. But how or why they acquired a demon side is beyond my understanding. I find it difficult to believe that Asmodeus would do such a thing."

"Yes, but how do the red dragon demons relate to these dragon hunters who Li told you to see?" Aisling asked.

Jian shrugged. "That's what I hope to find out. I feel obligated to meet with the dragon hunter himself to see if there is a connection."

"That sounds reasonable," Drake agreed.

I put my hand on Gabriel's leg, drawing strength

and comfort from the contact. "We were going home, but I feel like we should stay in London."

"On the contrary, little bird, we must hasten home immediately," Gabriel told me, covering my hand with his.

Aisling's brows rose. "Why? Your house in London is almost as strong as our Paris house, which—let me tell you—is a veritable fortress now that it's repaired from the last time Baltic blew it up."

Baltic's square flashed. "You were keeping my mate from me! Of course I blew it up."

"Pfft." Aisling dismissed the accusation. "You didn't even know she was here then. Anyway, let's not get distracted on that particular bugaboo. I gather from Gabriel's comment that we should be circling the wagons. Drake?"

"Yes," he answered. "I'm making arrangements now to gather the green dragons."

I leaned into Gabriel. "I guess we're off to Australia, then. Thank god for the Internet, so we can all stay in touch."

"Not that anyone has asked," Kostya said in a mildly aggrieved tone, "but I will return to Saint Petersburg with the black dragons."

"All seven of them?" Baltic asked.

Ysolde snorted with an attempt to keep from laughing.

Kostya glared at the screen. "There are more of us than of you blight dragons."

"LIGHT dragons!" Baltic snapped.

"So that's it, then," Aisling said, still looking thoughtful. "We gather our septs together while we're waiting to hear what Jim finds in Abaddon, and whether or not Jian is successful in finding this dragon hunter person. Is there anything else to discuss? I'm going to have to visit the little Guardians' room soon, and I hate to be that person sitting on the toilet while video chatting."

Drake cleared his throat. "I hesitate to say this, because I know Aisling will storm into my study scattering dire threats of Guardian retribution if I don't explain everything to her, but if we are facing a direct threat by Asmodeus, we need the ring."

"What ring?" I asked.

"I do not scatter dire threats of Guardian retribution casually, you know, dragon boy," Aisling said with a snort of her own. "And yeah, what ring? Is it, like, the One Ring? Hang on, no one say anything important. I'll be right back." Aisling disappeared from view.

Gabriel gave a nod. "Asmodeus's ring! I had forgotten about that. Drake makes an excellent point. Locating the ring should be a first priority. I believe, little bird, we may need to speak with Sally again."

My spirits dropped. "Really? Why?"

"Because as one-half of the Sovereign, there is not much she does not know." He gave my fingers a gentle squeeze. "The location of such a powerful talisman as Asmodeus's ring is probably within her purview."

I gave him a long look. "All right, but if she touches your thighs again, I really will get stabby."

"Boy, the things I miss while I'm dashing to the bathroom." Aisling hove into view again. "I want to hear all about Gabriel's thighs."

Drake's eyes narrowed. "You do not."

"Yes, I do. Also, you're adorable when you're jealous."

Drake ignored the kiss she blew to him. "I won't even dignify that with a response. So, as it stands now, Jian will ascertain the existence or not of a dragon hunter in the US, and his or her possible connection to the hybrids we saw. Aisling will send Jim into Abaddon to locate information there about what sort of curse Asmodeus is working on, and Gabriel and May will speak with Sally in order to locate Asmodeus's ring. Bastian, I assume you and Kostya will be looking to your respective kin."

"They are foremost in my mind, yes," Bastian said, nodding. "So few of them remain after the sundering by Fiat, but I have sent out word that we are to gather in Italy. In addition, the blue dragons wish to offer assistance to the other septs should they need to hire extra protection for their members."

"What sort of protection?" I asked. "Like … magic? Mages? Oracles?"

"If you felt that was necessary, although I was thinking more of a mercenary army that could be hired to protect vulnerable members." Bastian gave a half shrug. "I have already offered Jian protection for the few remaining members of his sept, but I would like to extend that to everyone."

"Sadly, there are only four of us altogether," Jian said, making another of his vague gestures that spoke so clearly of the tragedy he faced. "Although I much appreciate the offer, we four are together, and as safe as we can be."

Aisling sniffled, dabbed at her eyes again, and muttered something about pregnancy hormones before adding, "That's awfully sweet of you to include all the other septs, Bastian, but I'm sure if Drake felt we needed mercenary help, he'd be able to pay them. Without any undue bragging, he's rich as Croesus."

"*Kincsem!*" The look Drake shot his mate made me stifle a laugh, and pat Gabriel's leg again. He had just as fierce a temper but much better control of it than Drake and Kostya.

"Well, you are," Aisling said.

"Honestly, I doubt if he is as wealthy as the blue dragons." Ysolde's image shifted and bobbled as she obviously lifted her tablet and moved over to a bed with a massive headboard carved with fantastical dragons.

Aisling's eyes widened. "Really? Er … I hate to sound crass. …"

"Oh yes. They've always been stinking rich, and had lairs that were the envy of all the other septs, and I assume that has not changed," Ysolde answered as she settled on the bed, clearly propping the tablet up on her legs.

"Wow, I had no idea," I said, glancing at Gabriel. He looked thoughtful.

"Me either." Aisling smiled brightly at everyone. "Well, I was going to say that we should be the ones offering financial help if people need it, but if Bastian is sitting more than pretty, then I won't."

Bastian smiled, but said nothing.

"As for the game plan … Baltic and I will try to contact the First Dragon again and see if we can't pump him for more information," Ysolde said.

There was another disgusted snort from Baltic's now almost entirely black square. The interior lights of the car must be off. "You must know another Baltic, for I certainly have no intention of speaking with the First Dragon."

Ysolde waved a hand. "Don't be obstinate. We need to talk to him again now that we know the full score."

"The First Dragon is not one to be summoned and made to give information at your whim, mate," he warned.

She gave a twitch of her shoulder. "True, but maddening as he is, he can't want to see his descendants destroyed."

I had been thinking about the visit of the First Dragon, and said, "You know … it strikes me that if he came to warn you, that's a good sign that he is willing to discuss the issue. Because otherwise, wouldn't he have just sent you one of those visions that you used to get, Ysolde?"

"Fortunately, he stopped doing that right after he found out I was going to have Anduin." She glared past the tablet at what I assumed were her puffy ankles.

"I agree with May's assessment of the First Dragon's visits," Aisling said. "Kostya, is there something you can do?"

Kostya, who had been slumped back in a tall wingback leather chair, scowled at the camera. "I resent the implication that ensuring the members of my sept are safe from whatever threat Asmodeus poses is doing nothing."

"It goes without saying that you will take care of your own sept," Aisling said soothingly. "I was speaking of what you could do to help the weyr. Maybe help look for this ring that everyone thinks is so important?"

Kostya bristled at that, just as I knew he would. "Do I look like a hobbit that I have even the slightest idea how to find such a thing?"

"Well, you are kind of hairy," she said, her lips twitching. Beside her, Jim, who had clearly been ordered back to silence, bobbed its head with laughter.

"I am not hairy!" Kostya almost yelled. "I am a dragon!"

"Maybe hairy isn't the right word," Aisling temporized. "You have black hair, though, and that always makes men's toes look … well … hirsute."

A little curl of smoke wafted out of Kostya's left nostril. "Drake, would you please inform your mate that I do not have hobbit toes?"

Drake looked unimpressed with the whole conversation. "Frankly, I'm surprised you know what a hobbit is. I was introduced to them because Aisling insists the twins be seeped in mortal culture. Also, she has an unnatural passion for an actor named Viggo."

"It's not unnatural, and he wasn't even in the Hobbit movies. I apologize if I've offended your delicate male sensibilities, Kostya, but to return to the point, how about you see what you can find out about the ring? Just in case Sally doesn't want to be forthcoming with info, which, if I remember her correctly, is quite likely," Aisling said.

Gabriel leaned back, pulling me tighter against him. "Sadly, you may well be correct. Although I took the fact that she sought to protect us as a good sign."

"That's because you don't know her like I do," I said, smiling at him before turning back to the laptop. "I second Kostya using whatever resources he has to find the ring."

"I don't know how to find the ring, not that I offered in the first place," Kostya snapped.

"Thirded," Ysolde said quickly, obviously ignoring *Robert's Rules of Order* by jumping straight to the result she wanted. "Motion carried. Kostya will either work with this Sally person or dig up someone to help him find out where the ring has gone."

The look Kostya gave the camera had another giggle rising up in me, and Gabriel's dimples flashing. "Baltic! Inform your mate that she is *not* in charge of my life."

Baltic's dark square flashed. "Do it yourself. Unless you're afraid of her."

I thought Kostya's eyes might shoot lasers at the screen, but since that was a normal state with him, I did nothing more than pretend to cough to cover my laugh.

"I fear no woman!" he snarled.

"Dude," Ysolde drawled. "Get over yourself."

"You will not speak to me in such a manner. I am a wyvern," he said, his words sounding as if they were ground between two rocks.

Ysolde smiled. "And yet I vividly remember you a few hundred years ago being chased buck naked through a town by an irate mortal husband who swore he was going to geld you after he caught you shtupping his wife. Now, can we move past all the posturing? Was there anything else?"

Kostya's eyes first widened, then narrowed in fury, but he managed to keep from continuing on with his dramafest.

"I will deposit some funds in the weyr bank so that it is available when needed. Also, I have a connection with a revenant group who have recently started hiring themselves out as protection. I will engage the group and divide them up amongst the septs as additional support," Bastian offered.

Aisling nodded her approval. "I'm sure everyone appreciates that. Well, sounds like we have a plan of action. Or many plans of action. Sweetie, did you want to go ahead with calling another sárkány?"

"Yes," Drake said slowly. "I think that two weeks will be sufficient for everyone to accomplish their missions. Shall we meet in Paris at the end of that time?"

"I'm agreeable with that plan," Gabriel said.

Bastian nodded. "Yes. That should give me sufficient time to undertake my tasks."

"I don't know how the hell I'm supposed to find a ring that I know nothing about," Kostya complained. "However, I will do what I can."

Baltic's square blinked. "Ysolde will not attend the sárkány. She is recovering from childbirth."

"Don't even think of saying that to me in person," she said with a pointed look at the screen, then smiled. "We'll be there with bells on our nonhairy toes, everyone."

Jian took a long, slow breath. "Assuming I'm finished locating the dragon hunter, I, too, will be present for the sárkány. And *bonne chance* to us all."

"Amen to that," Aisling said, giving another wet sniffle before taking the tissue Jim dropped on her lap.

My dear Friia,

I assume these "warm fuzzies" you offered in your last message are intended to comfort me. If so, I thank you for the sentiment, as well as your offer of assistance. I fear a great sorrow is to be visited upon one of my children should the dark battle within him triumph, but I am unable to see how any of us can help him. Regardless, I will see that he will not be alone.

Your devoted brother,
First Dragon

SEVEN

THE CHAPTER THAT MAKES EVERYONE CRY

The trip to Seattle started out about as Jian Tin had expected—frustrating.

"You haven't heard of any dragon hunter in the area?" he asked his informant, hoping Mak, his second-in-command, was having better luck in Los Angeles.

The scryer looked up from her basalt bowl and shook her head. "I see no such person in the area."

Jian sighed to himself, and stifled the desire to rail against the time wasted in the Pacific Northwest. He thanked the woman and turned to leave when she, rotating the stone bowl in her hands, added, "There is something ... no, I don't think it's what you want."

"A dragon?" Jian asked, pausing at the door to look back at the scryer. She continued to stare into the bowl, gently rotating it as if it would clear the vision that only she saw in the water within.

"No. And yet ... yes. No." She shook her head again, looking up to give him a wry smile. "I'm sorry, that doesn't make any sense, does it? The one I see is hidden in shadows. I thought at first he was a dragon, but then felt the touch of cold about him that warned me he was filled with dark power."

"Where is this person?" Jian asked, deciding that he'd leave the area and head for San Francisco, the last on his list of potential locations for the dragon hunters. Perhaps if Mak was done searching Los Angeles, he could join him.

The scryer gave him an address, and Jian thanked her again before leaving.

He hesitated outside the scryer's home, flicking through his text messages, and an airlines app, quickly booking himself a flight to San Francisco that evening before looking up the address the scryer had given him.

It was less than an hour away.

I'm going to run down one final possibility here, but it would appear this was a massive waste of my time and money, he texted to Mak.

I know how you feel, Mak responded. *Everyone here is saying there were two dragon hunters who lived around here, but that was a few decades ago, and no one has seen them since. What do you want me to do?*

Meet me in San Francisco as soon as possible, he answered.

Will do. I'll check out the one whisper of dragons being seen in San Diego, then will fly up north and meet you tomorrow.

Dragons? What sept?

None that anyone recognized. I thought I'd check them out in case they are the missing dragon hunters. Shouldn't take much time.

Good luck, Jian responded, and got into the rental car, heading toward a small town at the foot of a nearby mountain range.

Jian had no sense of any danger as he approached the somewhat run-down single-story house. He was hungry, and desirous to leave the area so he could continue his hunt to track down those responsible for the deaths of his kin…

He stopped that thought even before it began, pushing down hard on the almost overwhelming pain mingled with fury.

He had to remain sharp, he told himself as he raised his hand to knock at the door. There was too much to be done to give in to emotions. Later, he would grieve. But now…

The door opened, and something hot and black and insidious seemed to envelop him, dragging him downward into an ebony pit of pain and nightmare.

"Sir? The plane has landed. I'm afraid you must disembark now."

Jian came to wit.h a start, his body jumping even as his dragon fire roared to life in response to what it perceived as an attack. Confused, he looked from the mildly concerned face of the woman bending over him to the rows of seats surrounding him.

He was on an airplane. He shook his head, trying to clear the confusion that seemed to leak from his brain like tar. "What? Oh. Yes. Of course." Even though he was feeling more than a little disoriented, he scooted out from where he had evidently been pressed against the airplane window, and started down the aisle, turning back when the flight attendant handed a bag to him that she said was his.

Three hours later, Mak arrived at the hotel where they had arranged to meet. Jian had spent the interval in denial, trying hard to ignore the fact that something felt wrong inside him. He was a wyvern, he told himself. Wyverns did not give in to trivial things like gaps in time that he couldn't recall.

But the blackness that now resided deep in his soul was undeniable.

"No," he told his reflection in the bathroom, shutting down the small kernel of fear in his belly. "I am a wyvern and a warrior. There is nothing that can overtake my dragon fire. Nothing."

"What's that?" Mak called from his bedroom. He emerged into the suite's living area, reading something on his phone.

Jian hesitated telling him that something had happened to him in Seattle, something he couldn't remember, but which had left him with a horrible sense of dread and despair.

And a darkness that he feared might overwhelm even the strongest of wyverns.

"Nothing," he said, deciding he'd leave a discussion of the missing time for later.

A half hour later, they started on a short list of possible contacts in San Francisco.

"I don't know how we're going to find this dragon hunter if he doesn't want to be found. I take it since you didn't mention much about your visit to Seattle that the trail there was cold?"

"You could say that." Jian was a warrior trained by Chuan Ren herself, and had never backed down from any fight. He shied away now from the weakness he feared might be inside him, helpless to articulate his fears.

Mak swore under his breath. "What more can we do? It's been a week and we're no closer to getting a definitive answer than when we got here."

Jian didn't look at Mak, his second-in-command. They'd been friends and compatriots almost since birth, despite both having fallen afoul of his adopted mother, Chuan Ren, more than once over the many centuries she'd been wyvern of the red sept. "We don't have much of a choice that I can see. It was our kin who turned into those monsters, even if they had left the sept before doing so. I could not hold up my head to the weyr should we have to bear that shame without having taken every possible action to get to the bottom of why they have so damned themselves in the eyes of the dragonkin. What is this place?"

Mak consulted his phone. "Chinatown. The thief taker said the dragon hunter was staying in this area of San Francisco."

"His name?" Jian glanced around, battling the sense of frustration that he should be chasing down someone who might not be who he said he was, along with the fury that members of his sept would so betray their own kind.

The dark, insidious presence shifted in his mind, leaving him momentarily gripped with a sense of panic and desperation.

"The thief taker? Er ..." Mak tapped a few times on his phone.

Jian fought against the dark need that seemed to grow with every passing hour. He closed his eyes for a few seconds, prodding once at the empty space in his memory, but it did not give up the secret he most wanted. "No, the dragon hunter."

"Ah. He is ... yes, here it is. Ian Iskandar." Mak looked up. "The thief taker wasn't sure if he was a dragon hunter, though. The last record he could find was dated more than a hundred years ago."

"Dragon hunters do not cease being what they are unless they are killed." Jian thought for a moment, remembering something Chuan Ren had once told him. "And then they can come back, if their espirits are so willing."

"Their what? Their spirits?"

He explained briefly all that he knew about the dragon hunter race. "It is the espirits that help their dragon selves overcome the demon inside."

The black presence stirred again. A strange, foreign emotion gripped him, making his palms sweat. He realized with a start that it was terror.

"Ah," Mak said, consulting his phone again. "Well, it is nothing to do with us if they are not part of the dragonkin."

"They aren't. They are separate, unique. Not even the ouroboros dragons claim—"

Jian was suddenly pushed forward, a sharp object poking into his kidneys. He spun around, his fire whirling within him, prepared to strike whoever had assaulted him, but the woman who faced him had an expression of utter surprise, followed immediately by chagrin.

"Oh, I am so sorry! Did I hurt you? I was trying to answer my phone, and the club got away from me. Here, let me look at your back—crap! There's a big smudge on the back of your jacket. I'm really sorry. I can try to wipe it off with a damp cloth, if you want to come into the office with me."

The woman gestured across the street. Jian eyed first a spiked club the likes of which he hadn't seen in a few hundred years, then the woman before him. She had a heart-shaped face, shoulder-length black hair that glistened in the afternoon sun like a raven's wing, and clear brown eyes flecked with black and gold.

Jian was no stranger to women despite his adopted mother's strictures against allowing his body to rule his mind, but there was something about this one that seemed to befuddle his sense. Without thinking, he took a step closer and breathed in her scent, the faintly spicy element of it sinking into his body and stirring his dragon fire. "Do not distress yourself," he told the woman when she raised one eyebrow at his lack of response. "I was merely startled, not injured. Er … would you mind if I asked why you are carrying a kanabo?"

She smiled, amusement lighting her eyes in a way that Jian felt to his toes. "You know what it is? Boy, are you in the minority. It's my boss's, actually. He had me fetch it from a welder who was repairing some of the spikes. I'm Sophea Long, by the way."

He gravely shook the hand she held out to him, delighted despite the situation in which he found himself. "Jian Tin." Mak, who had been standing to the side, cleared his throat in a very obvious way. Jian shot him a glance, but his friend's face was filled with amusement. "And this is Mak."

"Nice to meet you both," Sophea said, also shaking Mak's hand. "You don't sound like you are from around here. Oh hell. That sounds obnoxious, doesn't it? I didn't mean that there was anything wrong with not being from here. Or being from here and having an accent. I like your accent. It's nice." Sophea stopped, a faint blush pinkening her cheeks.

Jian was entranced. He'd never reacted to a woman—a mortal—the way he was reacting now. He wondered if whatever had happened to him in Seattle had affected him somehow. Regardless, he found himself answering, "We are not from the US, no. I live in Hong Kong most of the time."

"I prefer Singapore," Mak said, his gaze a little too full of admiration for Jian's taste.

"Do you?" Sophea asked politely.

"Yes, he does," Jian answered before his lieutenant could. "He's also just leaving."

"I am?" Mak asked, his lips twitching.

"You are. You were going to go to that address you mentioned."

Jian gave him a pointed look that had Mak, with a quick glance toward Sophea, giving him a mock salute. "Aye aye, mon capitaine."

"Are you a captain? A ship captain or navy?" Sophea asked when Mak, with a cheeky grin, finally took himself off. Jian breathed a sigh of relief, not sure why Mak's obvious admiration of Sophea suddenly irritated him so much. He'd never been overly possessive before, but there was something about Sophea …

"Jian?"

"Hmm?" With a start, he realized that she had asked him a question. "No, I am not a captain of any sort. Mak has a rather odd sense of humor."

"Well, as to that, so do I," Sophea said with a wry twist of her lips, gesturing with the kanabo. "I suppose if you aren't going to let me clean you—" She froze for a second, her cheeks turning a dark rose. "That is, if you aren't going to let me clean your coat, then I should go. It was nice meeting you. I hope you enjoy your stay in San Francisco. Er … this is going to sound a little weird, but if you need someone to show you around, I'm a qualified tour guide." She nodded toward the shop across the street. The windows were plastered with signs announcing that various walking tours of Chinatown were available. "Just … uh … in case you wanted to … you know … see the sights. Oh god. I'm babbling now."

He laughed, and made a decision that he didn't realize was there to be decided. He took her arm and, with a glance at the traffic, accompanied her across the street. "As it happens, I would love to learn more about this area, since I just arrived here. Do you provide private tours?"

She shook her head, sliding him a look from the corner of her eyes. "It's not allowed. For safety reasons, since most of the guides are women. But the daytime tours usually aren't too busy, if you had the time to join one now."

He didn't. He had a dragon hunter to find, any possible living sept members to track down, and demonic dragons to slay. "I would like that," he heard his mouth say, and gave a mental shake of his head. What was this madness? He wondered briefly at the immediate attraction he felt for Sophea, awareness of her prickling along his skin in a manner that was both irritating and arousing. Jian didn't normally dally with mortals, finding it wearisome to hide his true self, but it flashed into his mind that Sophea might well embrace his dragon nature, rather than run from it as most mortals did.

The text came at the end of the hour-long walking tour.

From: Mak

Checked out both the address the thief taker gave me and the one your contact in Seattle provided. Neither had what we seek. Are you with the mortal, or can we go to the oracle who you said charges exorbitant rates, but gets results?

To: Mak

Just finishing up a tour of the local area with Sophea. She's fascinating, and you can stop making that face that I know you're making. I don't have time for a dalliance. I was simply acquainting myself with this area, since it is always best to know the enemy's weaknesses.

From: Mak

That doesn't make the slightest bit of sense, and you know it. Just admit that you're interested in the mortal. You've been without a woman ever since ... well, at least there's no way Chuan Ren can kill this lover. Assuming you make the mortal so.

Jian glanced up from his phone to where Sophea stood in front of a cracked green door, describing a time in recent history when people were abducted and forced into labor on board ships.

"The term 'shanghaied' is now considered to be racially insensitive, but it is what the forced enslavements were called at the time," she announced to the small group of people, gesturing toward the door. "Men were conscripted from bars like the one through this door. Forcibly conscripted, usually by means of liquor, then they were rounded up by gangs who sold them to captains needing crew. Once on board a ship, they had a choice—work or get dumped into the sea."

Despite the grimness of her subject, Sophea's eyes sparkled with both humor and a joie de vivre that captivated Jian.

Her spirit shone, the gentle glow from it finding an answer in the dragon fire that simmered inside him.

The darkness shifted, tamping down part of his fire. For a few seconds, Jian panicked, his breath growing short as dread gripped him, leaving him impotent against its strength.

Light pierced the darkness, pushing it back a little. Sophea had stopped next to him, her eyes reflecting the smile that curved her lips. "You aren't going to tell me you're afraid to go down to the speakeasy, are you?"

With a desperate grab at his dragon fire, he pushed down the dark power, forcing his face into what he hoped was a pleasant expression. "I would go anywhere you desired."

Surprise flashed across her face, followed by another of those delightful blushes, but he could tell by the way she kept shooting him tantalizing little glances that she felt the shared attraction. The question was whether he should act on it now, or walk away from her.

Walking away would be the sane thing. He had work to do, the entire weyr was facing an unknown curse from the premiere prince of Abaddon, and he must find the dragon hunter reputed to be in the area before any more dragons suffered. He had no time for a woman, not even one as enticing as Sophea.

She filled his mind. Even as that thought struck him, he gave a little shake of his head. He'd never been one to allow his heart to lead his mind, and yet here he was, not just willing to forgo work for time with a mortal, but needing to do so. It was as if his future lay with the freckled, glossy-haired woman who blushed so delicately whenever she found his gaze on her.

"Come to dinner with me," he told Sophea a short while later, when he walked her back to the tour office. He glanced at his watch. "I have some work I must complete, but perhaps you can show me around other areas of San Francisco following dinner? Shall we say eight?"

Sophea's eyes glittered brightly. "I'd like that. Here, let me give you my address."

He gave her his phone, allowing her to make an entry with her information, his body demanding he do more now, but he was a wyvern. Despite his sudden—and almost overwhelming—attraction to Sophea, he must put the welfare of his sept and dragonkin ahead of fleeting moments of pleasure.

Two hours later, and having spent enough money to purchase a small condo in a recent development in the Hong Kong suburbs, Mak and Jian left the oracle's apartment.

"I hope she is right," Mak said as the two men retrieved their rental car from the parking lot. "I have a feeling you'd have a hard time getting a refund if this dragon hunter isn't where the oracle says he is."

"I am not worried about getting a refund," Jian said, his mind straying to Sophea. What was she doing now? It was almost six in the evening. Surely she had finished her shift at the tour company. Perhaps she was home now, bathing, preparing for their evening together. He dwelt with loving detail on how the warm water would lap at her breasts, making her skin silky and slick.

"That's only because you'll expect me to be the one to turn enforcer on her if she doesn't deliver," Mak said in a teasing tone that Jian ignored. He was too busy imagining himself standing with a large towel, helping Sophea dry off. "Then again, perhaps you'd like to eat a marshmallow pie."

"Perhaps," Jian said, wondering if he dared tell Sophea about his true nature before he took her to his bed, or if it was better to bring her into the world of dragonkin slowly, so as not to startle her.

Mortals so often had issues with the idea of the Otherworld, and he prided himself on being a thoughtful lover.

"Of course, if the dragon hunter turns out to be a caterpillar, then we are out of luck," Mak said.

No, he would wait to introduce her to his world. He owed that to her. He ignored the question of when he had decided that she was going to be a part of his life, and moved on to the how and when to rouse her to overwhelming passion. "If that happens, we will deal with it," he answered absently.

"I should find a mortal, too; then we can have an orgy."

"If you like." Jian narrowed his eyes at the idea that Sophea might not wish to tumble into his bed. Well, if she wanted wooing, then he would woo her to her heart's desire. He wondered what mortal men did when it came to romancing their mates, and stopped, looking long and hard at that word.

At what point had he stopped thinking of Sophea as a pretty woman and started thinking of her as a mate? A wyvern's mate was a rare thing—but she was mortal. And she was very attracted to him, more so than normal human women. He made a mental note to test her that evening with his dragon fire to see if she could withstand it. If so, he would have proof that she was his mate.

Mak's shout of laughter brought him out of a delightful reverie where Sophea was lying on his bed, covered in nothing but his dragon fire. He looked over at his friend, wondering if he had succumbed to some spell while they were visiting the expensive oracle. "Why are you laughing like a deranged person?"

"No reason," Mak said, wiping an eye and grinning broadly.

Jian gave him what he thought of as his sternest look, then reluctantly tucked thoughts of Sophea away in order to focus on what was important—speaking with the dragon hunter.

Warmth, thick and black, swept over him. His dragon fire tried to answer, but the blackness was too strong for it, swamping him, sucking him down into its inky depths until it consumed every thought.

"Jian!" It was his own name that penetrated the darkness, followed by a shock of cold that had him gasping for air, struggling to sit up even as he sputtered and spat out a mouthful of water. "Jian, are you—there you are. Are you all right? I thought you'd dozed off for a few minutes until I tried to rouse you. Your eyes—" Mak's gaze was filled with concern.

"What about my eyes?" Jian asked, realizing he was sitting on the warm asphalt of a parking lot, his upper torso and head wet. Next to Mak sat a battered orange plastic bucket. With a slightly shaking hand, Jian reached up to touch the edge of his face.

"They were … changed. Almost black." Mak helped him to his feet, brushing him off and pulling a small bag from the back seat of the car. Jian removed his wet shirt, used the dry lower section of it to mop up his head and hair, and quickly donned the scarlet shirt Mak had pulled from the bag. "What's going on? Don't look at me like that—something's been off ever since you came back from Seattle. Did you faint just now?"

"I don't know," Jian said slowly, his blood chilling at the thought that whatever blackness was within him was growing stronger with each passing hour. "And I don't know."

"You don't know if you fainted?" Mak asked, pressing the point.

Jian shook his head. "I don't know what happened in Seattle. I was … I lost time there. One moment I checking out the last lead I had, and the next I was waking up on the plane."

Mak watched him closely. Jian, for the first time in his life, could not bear for his old friend to look deeply into his eyes. He might see the blackness that now dwelt within. He turned away and, without another word, started toward the building in which the oracle had sworn he'd find the dragon hunter.

"Jian—" Mak started to say in a voice filled with warning, but Jian heard the thread of worry, and gestured toward his old friend.

"Not now. Later. First, let us deal with this dragon hunter. Then I must see about claiming Sophea. After that …" He stopped, unable to see past the idea that now obsessed his brain.

Sophea must be his. Only then would she be safe.

"Claim? You don't mean she's a mate?"

"Possibly. Probably. I've never had this reaction to a mortal woman before. Or a dragon, for that matter. What number?"

"Twenty-three. Jian—"

Jian punched the button under the appropriate box, and entered the building when the door buzzed. "I know, but we will have to talk about it later. For now, let us focus on this matter."

Mak shot him a look filled with meaning, but said nothing more on the subject as they climbed the two flights of stairs.

Voices could be heard even before they stopped at the appropriate door.

"—don't know who sent you, but I assure you that I do not need you," a man said.

Jian cocked an eyebrow at Mak, who had his hand raised to knock.

"See, that's what I'm talking about. You're so closed up! Just like a book that's bound with those little leather belts that look so adorable, but really are a pain when it comes to trying to make the book fit nicely in a shelf. Are those your kitties? I love kitties!" a female voice answered, trailing off into the sort of cooing noises that women made when faced with small, adorable balls of fluff.

Jian pushed open the door, which had been cracked a few inches, and strode into the room, his dragon fire riding high for some reason.

Inside, a tall man with dark hair and gray eyes stood scowling at a young woman, one who appeared to be eighteen or nineteen.

No, not a young woman. Jian narrowed his eyes at the girl as she whirled around, her hair, which was tied in blobs on the top of her head, bobbing merrily as she clapped her hands at the sight of them. This was no mortal being. She fairly glowed with light. And the man ... his gaze shifted. He was definitely not mortal.

"Oh goody! More dragons! You guys are just in time. You can tell Ian that he needs me," the young woman said, grinning at them.

"You are the dragon hunter?" Jian asked the man, considering him. He didn't bear any of the telltale signs he was a demon. "You are Iskandar?"

A martyred look crossed the man's face. "I am Ian Iskandar, yes. And you, sprite—"

"Former sprite," the young woman said, spinning around again so that her black-and-white striped short skirt twirled outward. "Now I'm ... well, I'm in training. Sally says I need a familiarity with all the important jobs that touch mortals, so here I am! Plus, she said you are going to need me to keep a big bad from happening."

"A big bad?" Jian asked before the man Ian could. "Do you refer to the curse Asmodeus is placing on dragonkin?"

"Nope," she answered, patting Ian on the arm. "This is something else. I'm Sasha. What's your name?"

"Jian, wyvern of the red dragons," he said, making her a bow.

"Awww," she said, her joyous expression fading somewhat.

For some reason, Jian felt as if a cloud had just passed over the sun.

"I don't care who you are, or what you used to be," Ian told the girl. "I don't need your help. I'm not a dragon hunter any longer. I gave it up almost a century ago."

Sasha moved her gaze from Jian to Ian, her head tipping to the side as she said, "Yeah, you say that, and yet, you've spent all that time rescuing those who need help. That sounds like a dragon hunter to me."

"I've done no such thing, and I refuse to discuss the subject any longer," he answered, pinning Jian back with a gaze that said much about denial. "What is it you want, Jian of the red dragons?"

"I want to know about the demon-dragon hybrids that are said to have been seen here."

Ian frowned. "Other dragon hunters? There are only two others on the West Coast—a father and daughter."

"There are two others?" Mak asked, looking annoyed as he pulled out his phone and started entering a text message. "I'm going to have a discussion with the thief taker who swore there were only two in total on this side of the country."

"Not dragon hunters," Jian answered, watching Ian closely. Was the sense of despair he felt coming from

Ian … or did it have something to do with the darkness inside himself? "These are demons who were once dragons. They are no longer kin, whereas you …" He stopped, unsure of how to put his feelings into words.

"I am what?" Ian straightened up, his hand reaching toward his hip, his fingers flexing for a moment. Jian recognized the movement, having worn a sword at his side for many centuries before it was outmoded by mortal societal norms.

"You have the scent of kin about you," Jian said slowly. "At least, I can sense dragon, even if I could not identify your sept."

"My mother was ouroboros," Ian said abruptly, his expression shuttered. "As am I."

"Ah. That would explain it. The demon hybrids that we encountered were also not kin. The demon controls them, whereas it is clear that your dragon self is in control."

Sasha, who had both hands full of three small gray kittens, kissed them on each of their heads before handing them to Ian. "The problem is whether that's going to stick or not. And it's why he needs me."

To Jian's surprise, the man took the kittens absently, almost as if he didn't realize he had done so. "I know of no such beings," Ian said, ignoring Sasha and frowning at nothing. "Nor have I heard of any demons running amok on the West Coast. Especially not ones who were formerly dragons. Are you sure of their origin?"

"That they were members of my sept? Unfortunately, yes. They left when I was …" His gaze shifted momentarily to Mak, then back to Ian, who now had all three kittens tucked into one arm, and was petting them with his free hand. "… I was out of contact of the sept."

"Ouch," Sasha said, giving him a sympathetic glance. "It's never good when you get imprisoned because you lip off to your boss. I know. Sally gets really testy when I tell her that she's not running things right."

Jian looked at her in surprise for a few moments. "Did you know Chuan Ren?"

"Nope." She smiled, giving another twirl. "But one of my sisters was dating a red dragon, and she—the red dragon—had a lot of things to say about the wyvern. Sweet Zizi's nips, I have to run. I'll be back this evening, Ian, and then you can train me up as an apprentice dragon hunter, and we'll get things on track for you before Sally demands I go learn something else, 'K?"

She was out the door before Ian could do more than sputter a few protests.

"That was an interesting"—Mak looked at the open doorway—"cherub? Definitely from the Court of Divine Blood."

"Sprite, I think," Jian said, giving a little shake of his head. "Although she said former. Still, she had the mannerisms of a sprite."

"Sadly, it's much worse than that," Ian said with another fleeting martyred expression. "As for your situation—I can be of no help. I am not a dragon hunter any longer. I can pass along word to the two who are located on this coast, however, if you need help."

Jian hesitated. He had no desire to bring outsiders into the situation if there was no reason to involve them. "No," he said after a minute of thought. "If the hybrids are not attacking mortals or other beings than dragons, then it is a problem for the weyr. We must take care of it ourselves. If you happen to hear anything about them, however—"

Ian gave him a little bow. "I will be happy to tell you if I see any demons who fit the description."

Mak wanted to talk after they left, venting his spleen loudly about the trip to the US. "It's been a waste of time from start to finish," he all but growled as he took his place behind the wheel of the car, staring moodily out the front window at a red light. "It's especially frustrating since we could have been in Western Europe, trying to track down the demon hybrids the other septs saw."

"Drake and Kostya have more dragons available to them," Jian answered absently.

"Perhaps, but they aren't as driven to find them as we are." Mak said something rude under his breath as he drove through the crowded city streets. "Where are we to look next? The thief taker—who is clearly worthless since he didn't know about the third dragon hunter—said he could find nothing but the vaguest of rumors about any demon hybrids, let alone ones on this coast. Not that I have absolute faith in him, given his lack of information."

Jian felt cold. The blackness inside him, he realized with a prick of concern, had gone from a warm, insidious feeling, to one of almost deathly cold. He pulled on his dragon fire, feeling a profound sense of relief when it answered his call, filling him with its heat, driving away the blackness that was starting to seep into the edges of his mind.

"I am seeing Sophea tonight. Tomorrow—" He stopped, not knowing what he wanted to say.

"Tomorrow?" Mak asked, glancing quickly at him.

"Tomorrow I must seek a shaman. There is one down the coast an hour away," he said slowly. It was not unknown for dragonkin to seek aid outside of their own kind, but seldom did they have to resort to such extreme actions.

"A shaman?" Mak's voice was filled with surprise, but the next words were devoid of all emotion. "The missing time?"

"Yes." Jian stared sightlessly out of the window, wishing he knew why he felt such a desperate urge to bind Sophea to him. He preferred to woo slowly, to be sure of his partner before baring the truth of his nature. But Sophea was different, he told himself, pushing away the doubts and worries of the moment, embracing the thought of her light and laughter that had so caught him in their silken web. She was unlike any other woman.

* * *

Three days later Jian stood in front of a mirror as he adjusted the red-and-black tunic that he had donned for his wedding. Gossamer memories of the last seventy-two hours floated by and around him as he stared blindly at himself.

Images danced in his head of his first night with Sophea, that glorious night that started with dinner overlooking the water, and ended with them together in the massively oversized tub in his suite, Sophea giggling and rosy with the heat of the water, all the while covered in bubbles that slid enticingly down her silken flesh.

He'd had to rein in his dragon nature when she allowed him to make love to her, since he was determined to do things right by her. And amazingly, her presence seemed to drive the darkness inside of him away, filling him only with the fire that her passion had stirred.

"You really do have it bad," Mak said after Jian had spent two days with Sophea being guided around the various tourist spots in San Francisco (ones he had little to no interest in except that they allowed him to spend time with the woman who was fast entwining herself around his heart). "Are we going to stay, or go back home now that we've found what we were looking for?"

"We'll stay for a few more days," Jian said, making yet another snap decision. The idea of being parted from Sophea wasn't even open for consideration. But he wanted to woo her gently, without overwhelming her with the truth about the Otherworld. "Then we'll return home."

Mak cocked an eyebrow. Jian smiled. "Yes, with Sophea."

"You're going to tell her, then?"

"About who we are? I will. After we have the mortal marriage ceremony. What? Yes, I am coming." Jian gave Mak a meaningful look as he responded to Sophea's inquiry if he was ready for the day's expedition to a nearby island.

Jian gave no thought to whatever had happened to him in Seattle; either the darkness that had resulted was driven out by the shining light that was Sophea, or her presence had forced it into dormancy. He relaxed, and planned for the future. First, he would wed her as he knew she would expect, and then he would explain to her the nature of dragons, and his sept.

The following day, a giggling Sophea emerged from the great stone building that housed a registry office and courthouse, her hand tucked firmly onto the crook of his arm, her face filled with such joy and happiness that it made Jian want to shout from the highest point of the city that she was his.

He paused as Mak went down the steps to the sidewalk, and turned Sophea so that she faced him, pulling her hands up to kiss both palms. "And so it is done."

"You are crazy, you know that, right?" she asked, laughing even as she leaned in and brushed her lips on his. "Crazy, sexy, and so adorable. My friends are going to freak when I tell them we got married after knowing each other only a couple of days."

He bathed in the warmth of her eyes, grateful to the tips of his toes that she had come into his life, that she had chosen him of all beings to love. She was his. His glorious, joyous mate, who banished the horror within, and filled his life with laughter and love. "You are now blood of my blood, kin of my kin, Sophea Long. I so name you, and will cherish and honor you to the end of my days."

Her beautiful eyes turned liquid with love, the emotion wrapping around him in a manner that left him breathless, and swearing he would do whatever it took to protect her. "You say the most romantic things. I love you, Jian, with my heart and soul and everything that I am."

"You accept me, all of me?" he asked her, feeling the need for her to swear fealty even before he explained who he was, and that she was now a wyvern's mate. "Everything I am and will be?"

"Everything," she said on a breath that brushed his lips, and then she was in his arms, stirring his fire until he had to set her from him, lest it slip his control and manifest itself.

"Tonight," he said, allowing her to see the passion in his eyes.

"Oooh," she answered, then, with a laugh as Mak pulled the car up to the loading zone across the street, ran down the stairs, casting a come-hither glance over her shoulder.

He followed, his heart light despite the threat that loomed over them all. Just as they were crossing the street, he caught a movement from the corner of his eye and, without thinking, spun Sophea around and more or less flung her out of the way of the car that veered around a smaller vehicle, slamming into him with a force that took his breath away.

The sound of Sophea screaming was the last thing he heard, echoing in his mind for a very long time. At some point, he realized that it had changed, no longer a shriek of terror, but instead the high call of a bird somewhere overhead.

He opened his eyes, and found himself lying in a garden. A shadow flickered and suddenly, a man was before him. Jian scrambled to his feet, confused and feeling more than a little adrift. "Dragon sire?" he asked, making a less-than-elegant bow.

"Child of fire," the First Dragon said, stopping before him, his eyes glittering golden in the warm afternoon sun.

Jian glanced around, unsure of exactly where he was. Was this one of the visions with which the First Dragon had blessed Ysolde?

"No," the First Dragon answered just as if he'd asked the question aloud. "This is no vision. You are a wyvern, and I see all wyverns before they pass beyond."

With a horror, Jian remembered the car bearing down on him, and the noise of Sophea screaming his name. A lump tightened painfully in his throat. "I am dead, then?"

The First Dragon just looked at him, his eyes darkening to mahogany.

"Why? How? I … the car?" Jian had his answer even as the words left his lips.

The First Dragon placed a hand on his shoulder, offering sympathy that Jian didn't want to accept.

"My mate …" His voice cracked even as he felt the unfamiliar burn of tears. "I had a mate. Sophea. She just swore fealty to me. To the sept. She will be alone—I did not even have time to tell her who we were. Could you not send me back? I would like to break it to her slowly, so she is not overwhelmed."

The First Dragon said nothing, watching Jian closely, but he felt as if he had been judged and found wanting.

"I am cognizant that it is a great affront to even ask you for such a boon, but I have not had time to prepare my mate for life with the dragonkin. The red dragons who remain will care for her but—"

"My children of fire are no more," the First Dragon said, and for a moment, Jian staggered with the depth of sorrow that leached from him.

"Mak—my friend—he was with me—"

The First Dragon shook his head.

Jian wanted to rail and weep and rage against Fate, but he was a wyvern. "The other two members of my sept?" he asked in a voice that sounded strange to him.

"They are in hiding," the First Dragon answered, his eyes changing again, this time to a dark reddish brown.

"And what of the demons?" Jian asked. "The ones born of my sept—are they dead, too?"

The First Dragon closed his eyes, pain etched on his face. "No."

Jian dropped to his knees. "Then there is no hope for us."

"There is. The dragonkin must find the one who once was but is no more, before there will be peace in the weyr."

Jian was not a spiritual man, but his bond to the members of the red sept was as integral to him as was his dragon fire. "Do you see dragonkin when they pass from the mortal realm, too? Did my dragons know that I was proud of them? That I honored and respected all of them?"

"You were their wyvern, even if only for a short time," the First Dragon said with a gentleness that fell like a balm on the pain that gripped Jian. "They knew your love."

Jian bowed his head for a few moments, a supplicant before the only one who could help him. "Sophea. My mate. She is alone. Could you not send me back to see to her welfare? It wouldn't have to be long. Just a few days."

It was a full minute before the First Dragon replied. "Do you have that long?"

A lone tear slipped over his lashes. Jian had been raised to view weeping as a sign of weakness, but the thought of Mak and the members of his sept being destroyed, and of Sophea being left alone, was too much to bear. He touched a spot on his chest where he felt the darkness once again. Now that Sophea was gone, it had returned, and he knew the truth about it. He knew he had been killed because only Sophea was able to keep it at bay "You know?"

"If you could not be turned, you must be destroyed," the First Dragon said, speaking the words that whispered in Jian's head.

"Who did it to me? Who buried a demon in my soul? Why would they attack the red dragons in this way? What was the purpose for eliminating us?"

The First Dragon looked thoughtful for a few minutes before saying, "Mates are rare, and must be cherished. I will take up the matter of your mate. What do you want for her?"

"A protector," Jian said quickly, gratitude easing a little of the pain that laced him. "Someone to keep her safe. And … happy. She deserves to be happy. She has such joy of life. I want her to be happy."

"She is a wyvern's mate," the First Dragon pointed out.

Jian closed his eyes for a moment against the pain of what the First Dragon was asking. He'd just found Sophea, just found the happiness that had eluded him for the entirety of his life. "Yes," he finally said, his voice choked. "She is."

The First Dragon nodded. "So shall it be." He lifted his hand and brushed his thumb on Jian's chest. "Go, child of fire, without the darkness that was consuming you."

A great lightness filled Jian, a golden, brilliant light that burned out the darkness that was eating away at his soul. His heart cried out at the loss of his kin, and the woman who had claimed him body and soul, but he gave himself up to the First Dragon's light with a sense of contentment that surprised him.

Sophea would be well. She would be happy. He just hoped the First Dragon would find someone who would love her as much as he did.

He turned away from the First Dragon and the light, and went to meet the kin who had gone before him.

My dear Friia,

Your condolences are much appreciated, as was the destruction you and Óðinn wrought in revenge upon the demons you sought out and found.

My children are resilient. They will continue on, although I fear they have more trials before them.

Your devoted brother,
First Dragon

EIGHT

IN WHICH SASHA DOES HER THING, TO THE BEWILDERMENT OF ALL

"You know that bad feeling I had earlier? Well, it's gotten a hundred times worse."

Drake, standing next to me, watched with narrowed eyes when the former demon lord Magoth strolled into the large conference room of a Paris hotel. "Magoth does have that effect on people," he said, but I heard a thread of concern in his voice that had me taking his hand.

He glanced at me, aware that the gesture was mostly for comfort, but also to show him support since the news we anticipated wasn't particularly good.

"Do not fret, *kincsem*," he said softly, his fingers squeezing mine gently.

"I'm going to do a whole lot more than fret if Jim doesn't show up in the next thirty seconds," I said just as softly before releasing Drake's hand and saying loudly as I stomped forward, "Magoth, where's my demon?"

"May, my sweet one—" Magoth started undulating his way over to where May stood with Gabriel, but stopped when I whipped up a binding ward and flung it on him. "What is this outrage? I am a demon lord, one of the seven princes of Abaddon! I will not be treated thusly. You, green dragon, control your woman!"

"Oh, you do not talk over me like that," I snapped, stopping in front of him, my hands on my hips, and the meanest look I could muster on my face. In a couple of strides, Drake was at my side, since he is in überprotection mode now, and looked with magnificent menace at Magoth. "I am a Guardian, which you know well since I went into great detail about everything I would do to you if you mistreated Jim after I temporarily signed it over to your care. Where is it? Has it stopped to get something to eat? Please don't tell me you let it go to that horrible butcher two streets away that carries horsemeat. I've told Jim that it is confined strictly to those meats that I don't find personally repugnant, not that I don't find most everything but chicken fried rice repugnant these days, but that's just pregnancy hormones."

"Guardian, I demand that you unbind me," Magoth said with lofty disdain. His black-eyed gaze was haughty one moment, then suddenly switched into one of simmering seduction as he eyed me up and down. "Ah, you are with child? How I love a fecund female. They offer so much with so little risk of being obliged to account for offspring. You will soon be too plump to please your dragon, so you would no doubt like me to bring you those experiences that only I can provide, hmm? I have many things that we can do together, some that will bring you to the exquisite pinnacle of pleasure. Or pain, since it is often the same thing. Do you enjoy rough bedsport, Guardian? I can think of twelve different ways I can show you the thin line of difference between ecstasy and agony without harming the child in your belly."

I held Drake back with a hand when he growled deep in his chest, ignoring both the dragon fire I could feel rising in him and the little spurt of flame that burst around Magoth's expensive shoes. "OK, first, ew. And second, no one gets to exquisite pinnacle of pleasure me except Drake. And third, ew."

"You said that already," Magoth said with a sniff before tamping out the fire burning merrily around his feet. "Pregnancy has clearly muddled your mind."

"It bore repeating. No, sweetie, you don't need to beat Magoth within an inch of his wretched life. I need to find out from him where Jim is."

Magoth sniffed again, and studiously examined one of his fingernails. "I am not used to being treated in this cavalier manner. Bondage, yes, I am in complete support of bondage. Razor-bedecked leather straps and small, lightly barbed chains can never be displeasing to the connoisseur. But this? This Guardian ward is offensive on all levels. My sweet May will no doubt attest to the fact that I do not find such things at all titillating."

"Don't bring us into this," May said as she strolled over with Gabriel. "You know better than to mess with dragons and their mates, and that goes double when the mate in question is as powerful as Aisling. Where is Jim?"

"I find it difficult to focus when I am bound in this petty manner," Magoth said, waving a languid hand.

"I suppose I can release you, since you won't have to vacate the premises until Jian arrives, and the sárkány proper can start." With a sour look at Magoth, I broke the ward. "But you will answer the question about Jim, or I'll do far more than bind you with a ward. And no, it won't be anything you find particularly titillating."

"Jim?" Magoth asked, oozing his way over to the table holding libations. He moved with a particular grace all his own, more of a glide than anything else, but it didn't touch the way Drake walked, all coiled power and smoldering sexuality. "I know not of whom you speak. Bah. Dragon's blood. Undrinkable at best. Do you have no blood of a virgin? Juiced Australian Imp? No hemlock or even tincture of nightshade?"

"We're not here to provide you with food and beverage," May said with a frown. "Answer the question, please."

"There is tequila," Gabriel pointed out, momentarily distracted by a couple of bottles.

Dragons, I had found out over the years, had an inexplicable fondness for tequila when they couldn't get their preferred dragon's blood wine.

"That is always acceptable," Magoth said, taking up a bottle. "So long as I get the worm."

Drake snatched the bottle away just as the demon lord was about to swig it. "You will answer the question as to the demon Jim's location first."

Magoth glared at Drake. "I thought you were supposed to have manners. My sweet May always said dragons had the best manners. Taking my tequila worm is the opposite of manners, dragon."

"So is gelding, demon lord," Gabriel said, leaning in with almost as much menace as rolled off Drake.

"You have two seconds to tell me where Jim is, and if you don't, I will send you to the Akasha," I told Magoth, dispensing a potent glare of my own. "One one thousand, two one thousand."

"I don't know!" Magoth snapped, taking a big swig from a second bottle of tequila. "Ask the mage that Asmodeus had imprisoned." He paused to say in an aside to May, "You would not believe what Asmodeus has done to my former palace. He stripped all the marble tiles and replaced them with lava flows. Actual streams of molten, fiery rock moving down the hallways. Do you have any idea how hard it is to get dried lava off of leather boots?"

May looked startled, but didn't answer before I swore. "For Pete's sake, Magoth! You lost Jim? How could you lose it? It's bound to you!"

"Can't you just"—May waved her hand in a vague gesture—"summon Jim?"

"It was bound to me," Magoth told me, filling my gut with a cold dread. He contemplated the tequila bottle for a few seconds before adding, "I bartered it away to the mage when three of Asmodeus's wrath demons recognized me and went running to their master to tell their tales. The mage agreed to get me out of Abaddon in exchange for the demon Effrijim."

I stared at him for a moment, horror stripping words from my tongue long enough for Gabriel and Drake to be in place to stop me when, inevitably, I attempted to throttle Magoth.

"Just let me kill him a little bit," I grunted, struggling with Drake, who had managed to pry my fingers off the neck of the squawking Magoth. "Just a tiny bit of death. Not enough to really bother anyone. I swear I'll just strangle him a little bit to death, and then it'll all be fine."

"Aisling, no," Drake insisted, gently but persistently pulling me from where Magoth had attempted to swoon on Gabriel, but a fast side step by the latter ended up with Magoth hitting the floor. "I know you are upset—"

"Upset?" I switched my glare from the demon lord to the man I loved. "Drake, he gave away Jim! He just handed it over to god knows who—"

"The mage's name is Helath," Magoth wheezed, managing to snag the bottle of tequila as he sat up.

"—so that Jim can be tortured or possibly even killed!" I finished, clutching at Drake's arms when they stopped confining me and moved around me in a gesture of love. Tears spilled down over my lashes as a thousand horrible images danced through my mind.

"The demon can't be killed, which you know full well," Drake said in his annoyingly calm voice, one hand stroking my back. "*Kincsem*, you will do yourself a harm if you give in to such violent emotions. Think—Jim is smart. It will not allow itself to be hurt. If it allowed Magoth to bind it to the mage, it must have done so for a reason."

I blinked up at him through my tears. "You really think so?"

There was nothing but love shining in those gorgeous green eyes. "I never thought I'd find myself saying this, but Jim loves you too much to allow itself to be parted from you for long. There must be a reason it went willingly with the mage."

I looked over at Magoth, who had propped himself up against the wall the better to drink the tequila. "Is that true, Magoth? Did Jim allow you to give it to this Helath without making a fuss?"

Magoth waggled a hand, and belched. "It whined a great deal about there being no cheeseburgers available in Abaddon, but it did not grovel and beg for mercy, if that is what you are asking."

I slumped against Drake, relief swamping my overwrought imagination. "Well, thank the stars for that."

"I'm sure Jim is fine," May said, stepping over Magoth to give me a sympathetic pat on the arm. "It's been around for a long time, and can take care of itself, even in Abaddon."

"I know. I just worry. I'm a mother," I said, realizing just how ridiculous that sounded, but luckily, no one commented on that.

Kostya, who had been at the far end of the room having an argument with Baltic while Bastian conversed with Ysolde, evidently realized that he was missing out on the opportunity to fight with Magoth, for he hurried over to us, followed by the others.

"What's going on? Is Magoth being annoying? Drake looks like he wants to spit, which tells me that, yes, Magoth is being annoying," Ysolde said.

"Are we fighting?" Kostya cracked his knuckles as he glared at first Magoth, then Gabriel. "Are we picking sides, or going for a full-on melee scrimmage? I pick Drake if we're doing teams."

"No one is fighting," I started to say, but was instantly drowned out by Baltic announcing that he needed no one on his team, and that he'd be happy to take on both Kostya and Drake by himself.

"I am, by rule, a lover, not a fighter, but I will be happy to join in," Bastian said, removing his midnight-blue coat and loosening his tie. "Teams of two? Gabriel, shall we?"

"I'm game—" Gabriel would have said more, but Ysolde, as senior mate, and thus the one with the most experience in quelling tempers, put her foot down.

"There will be no fighting! This pissing match is over before it begins, do you all hear me? There are no teams, no scrimmage, and no pig-piling on Baltic, and don't you dare try to look innocent, Kostya

Fekete, because I know full well that's what you are thinking."

"I wonder if Pavel can get here in time to pick up the pieces of the other wyverns," Baltic mused, pulling out his phone. The guards had all been banned from the sárkány, since we weren't sure what we'd be presenting to the respective septs, and I knew they'd all gone to hang out at G&T. The premiere club for all members of the Paris Otherworld was, naturally, being watched, but thus far, the demon dragons had kept away.

Ysolde sent Baltic a particularly scathing look that he summarily ignored. "Oh for heaven's sake ... ladies! Please tell them we don't have time for them to indulge in this."

"You know," I said slowly, eyeing Drake. Now that I was calmer in my mind about Jim, I could feel the tension humming in the air. "Much though I don't get off on boxing or that sort of thing, I think that perhaps we could allow them a short amount of time to work off a little steam. The tiny bit of throttling I got in on Magoth did me a world of good."

May pursed her lips as she considered Gabriel, who had a hopeful look in his eyes. "Everyone has been pretty on edge and jumpy lately. I suppose it wouldn't do any harm so long as you guys didn't seriously hurt each other."

The two women looked at me. "Normally, I'd say they could just tough it out, but knowing how much these guys love a good fistfight—and how much it tension it releases—I'm going to give the idea of a short brawl my OK."

Drake and Kostya looked downright pleased.

Ysolde's shoulders slumped, but she moved over to take a chair next to me, waving wanly at where the dragons were even now squaring off. "Far be it from me to be the reasonable one and ask that everyone behave in a civilized manner. Just don't come crying to me when your collarbones are all smashed to smithereens."

"Gabriel will fix everyone up," May said complacently as she, too, sat next to me.

"What weapons are we using?" Magoth asked, draining the bottle of tequila and smashing it on the edge of the table.

"No weapons!" Ysolde and I yelled at the same time.

"Also, no dragon form," May added, frowning at Kostya, whose arms were shiny and black with scales.

He made a disgusted face, but returned to normal.

"Put the bottle down, or you don't get to play with the rest of the boys, Magoth," Ysolde told the demon lord, who pouted slightly.

"I don't have a team," he said, pointing at where Bastian and Gabriel, and Drake and Kostya, were each quietly consulting as they stripped off their coats and ties, as well as rolling up their sleeves.

"You can have Baltic," she answered, gesturing at the man in question.

"The hell he can!" Baltic snarled. He'd removed his shirt altogether, and I had to admit, his famed six-pack was almost as nice as Drake's chest and belly.

"Mate," Drake said with an obvious warning tone in his voice.

"I was just looking," I said indignantly, damning the fact that he'd caught me ogling Baltic's bare chest. "Stop making that face at me—I'm pregnant! It's the hormones making me look."

The other five men in the room all turned to look at Baltic, who raised his eyebrows, and instantly, the room was full of shirtless men.

"I have to say, there isn't anything at all wrong with that picture," I said sotto voce to May and Ysolde as the men formed the rough outline of a circle.

"You can say that again," Ysolde murmured, then raised her voice, and added, "You have ten minutes! Barefisted fighting only. Please do not knock out any teeth. If you are injured, Gabriel will have to attend to you, and we will make him use his magic saliva on you. *From the source.*" The emphasis of her words was unmistakable.

The men all looked at Gabriel with the same expression of disbelief and mild horror that he, himself, bore.

Except Magoth, who promptly shucked all his clothing, smiled wickedly at Gabriel, and then moved over to stand next to Baltic.

Baltic gave him an outraged look, then glared at Ysolde. "Mate!"

"If you don't have a partner, you can't participate," she told him. "By yourself, the others would all jump you, and then I'd get mad and have to start throwing magic at them, and we all know how that will turn out."

"Bananas," May said, nodding.

"Fine, but he has to put his trousers back on," Baltic said, giving Magoth's cursed penis a disparaging glance.

"You really know how to take the fun out of fisticuffs," Magoth told him, but yanked on the tight leather pants that clung impossibly low on his hips, so low that they just about bared all.

"It goes without saying that everyone will behave, or they will have to go sit in the time-out corner," I said loudly. "Ready? On thr—"

I didn't even get the word out before there was a mass rush of men flinging themselves on one another.

Ysolde and May and I watched for a few minutes to make sure that no one was ganging up unfairly on anyone else, and then consulted one another on what was best to do about the curse situation.

"Is there any way you can contact Jim, even if you can't summon it?" May asked, applauding lightly when Gabriel knocked Kostya down. Drake, who was spinning around with Bastian clinging to his back, flung himself onto Gabriel, and all three men crashed down on top of Kostya.

"That's a good question," I asked, thinking about it. "Normally I would say I could just call it, but obviously, I can't."

"Why can't you?" Ysolde asked.

I watched Drake rise up from the ground, a stream of blood trickling from his mouth. His hair was mussed, and his eyes blazed with a liquid emerald light, but I could tell he was enjoying himself greatly. Kostya and he turned back to back to defend themselves from a sudden onslaught of the other three dragons and Magoth.

"It's in Abaddon," I answered Ysolde, wincing when Drake, under the mistaken belief that the man who thumped into him was an attacker, punched his brother dead in the eye, sending Kostya's head snapping back. "I'm not sure where he is. Phones are OK in parts of Abaddon, like Asmodeus' palace, but in other parts, there's no cell phone coverage."

"There isn't?" May asked, applauding again when Gabriel took advantage of Drake's mistaken attack on Kostya and kicked the back of his knee until he staggered forward into Magoth. "Are you sure?"

"My phone certainly never worked when I was there and outside of a palace," I answered, raising my voice to say, "Baltic, please don't hurt anything important on Drake. We might want more kids later."

Baltic, who was indeed looking like he was about to go for a vulnerable spot, scowled at me.

Ysolde blew him a kiss. "The same goes for us, my love."

He was so distracted by that comment that all four dragons turned and rushed him. Magoth squealed with delight, and hurled himself on top of the pile that resulted.

"I know for a fact that Magoth used to be able to call out of Abaddon when he was in residence, even outside of his domicile," May said, frowning when Magoth and Gabriel rolled to the side, the former getting in what sounded like a crunching blow. Fire erupted around the former demon lord.

"No fire," all three of us said in unison.

"Hmm," I said. "I wonder if things have changed."

"I'll ask," May offered, and stood up to yell, "Magoth, is there mobile phone coverage in Abaddon outside of the palaces?"

Magoth's head popped up. One eye was swollen and closed, his hair stood on end as if he'd stuck a fork in a light socket, and the left side of his chest was singed black from Gabriel's fire. "Of course. Asmodeus may be many things, but he installed Wi-Fi throughout Abaddon as soon as he could force a provider to his will. You dare! That was my favorite patch of pubic hair!"

This last was spoken to Bastian, who rose out of the pile with a horrified look at a small black clump of hair clutched in his fist. He hastily shook it from his hand and went down into the general kerfuffle when Magoth tackled him at the knees.

"Well, that's interesting."

"Not really," May said with complacence. "Magoth has a very high regard for all of his pubic hair. He uses a variety of unguents and oils to keep it in what he calls prime form."

"No, not his short and curlies—although really, can't the man wear pants that go high enough to cover that up?—but that Asmodeus had Internet service provided throughout Abaddon. Well, I guess there's one way to find out if that's true or not." I pulled out my phone and dialed Jim, glaring at Bastian and Gabriel when they, evidently in accord with Baltic, went after Drake. I ignored the muffled grunts and quite audible curses in what I knew was Zilant, the language of the dragons before English was adopted, and counted the rings.

Just as I thought Jim's voice mail was going to pick up, a familiar voice said, "Yo, babe!"

"Jim! Oh, thank god you're OK. Magoth had us worried when he said he traded you away. Where are you? What are you doing? Are you finding out anything about the curse? Are you eating all right?"

"Where you left me, answering your call, a little, and not even close. They like their meat raw here. Can you believe that? Raw! I'm fine with a bit of sushi now and again, but not just a slab of raw flank tossed on the floor. Would it kill them to get in a few grills so we could eat like civilized demons?"

I put my hand over the lower half of my phone, relief filling me. "Jim's fine," I told May and Ysolde, both of whom were watching me closely. "It's bitching about the lack of grilled meats."

"Sounds like Jim," May said with a smile. "I'm glad to know it's all right."

"What are you doing?" Jim asked, its voice sounding a bit winded. "Why do I hear someone yelling that

Drake's mother was a three-legged whore? Did Catalina get another leg and no one told me? Man, I miss everything!"

"You're not missing anything other than the men having a few minutes of tension releasing—Gabriel, I saw that! You should be ashamed of yourself! If you have to lick Drake's nose to make it better, you have no one to blame but yourself."

May giggled, but quickly schooled her expression into one of solemnity when I turned my look of outrage on her.

"Fires of Abaddon, Aisling! You're having a full-on fight fest with Gabriel licking people, and I'm not there? I hope at the very least you're filming it for me," Jim complained.

"What are you doing other than eating raw meat, which I hope you're being careful with, because I don't want you getting worms? Have you found out just what Asmodeus is doing? Why is he cursing us? And most importantly, when? How? Where?"

"Ixnay on the estionsquay," Jim answered in a hushed tone before saying in a louder tone, "Right, right, so you want a full case of barbed whips and two dozen nipple clamps sent off immediately to Asmodeus's HQ. Gotcha. Will do."

"You're not alone, are you?" I asked, worried about my furry little demon, but at the same time, oddly proud that it was braving Abaddon by itself.

"Nope, but it's OK. I got this," it whispered, then added in a normal tone. "Heya, Helath. Back from tormenting imps early, eh?"

The phone clicked off, and after a moment of wishing I could have Jim back by my side, I gave a watery smile to the others. "You heard?"

"Jim will be fine," Ysolde said, giving my arm a sympathetic pat.

"It sounds like it has everything under control," May added.

I sniffed back a few tears, then glanced over to see how the men were doing.

"That's it, your ten minutes of complimentary beating each other to a pulp is up," Ysolde said, rising and bustling over to tsk over the cut on Baltic's chin, which had splattered blood on his chest.

The men, all of whom were panting, their chests and faces damp with sweat, backed away from one another, four of the five of them with limping gaits. The fifth, Kostya, teetered forward a few steps, then collapsed onto a chair. In the center of the floor, facedown—and apparently unconscious—lay Magoth.

"Well, now that the testosterone hour is over, let's see how much licking Gabriel has to do," I said, moving over to examine Drake. Other than a torn lip, he didn't look too damaged, although there was a faint bruise over one eye, and the fingers of his right hand were swollen.

"I refused to be licked," Baltic said in an antagonistic manner as Ysolde dabbed at his chin cut. "Not by the silver wyvern, at least."

Kostya waved a hand as if he was going to speak, then slid off the chair with a whumping noise.

"He can lick me," came a muffled voice from where Magoth lay with his face against the floor. "Although I won't enjoy it until the internal bleeding stops."

"There will be no—Mayling, please, that tooth is not loose, just swollen, and you pressing on it to see if you can wiggle it is making it more so—there will be no licking on my part," Gabriel said, slumping back in the chair where May had pushed him.

I handed Drake a couple of tissues, decided Bastian—who was trying to flex one shoulder and having difficulty doing so—needed more help than I was able to give him, and went to fetch the bottle of dragon's blood wine, distributing glasses of it to all the dragons present.

"Would you mind popping Bastian's shoulder back into the socket?" I asked Gabriel as I handed him the glass. "I imagine it's pinching a bit being dislocated."

"My head is broken," Kostya said, clawing his way into an upright state so he could accept the wine. He sipped gingerly, wincing. "I hope there's more than one bottle of that left."

"If you boys wouldn't insist on fighting each other, you wouldn't be sitting here now having your shoulders—ouch, I could have done without that sound, Gabriel—being shoved back into their sockets."

Gabriel, who waited while Bastian moved his arm back and forth before nodding and drinking heavily from the goblet of wine, paused. He glanced at his watch, and asked, "Has anyone heard from Jian? The sárkány was due to start half an hour ago, and it is not like him to be absent without sending a message."

There was a few minutes where everyone—with many muffled groans and muttered invectives—checked their respective phones, but the last text received had been one four days before, acknowledging the date and time of the sárkány.

"Will you start without him?" I asked Drake.

He frowned at his phone, not having received a response to the text he'd sent asking for Jian's ETA. "I dislike doing so, but we may need to once we dismiss the demon lord."

"Which is my cue," I said, moving in to stand next to May. "Right, Magoth, since Jim was unable to talk, it's time for you to earn all that money that Gabriel paid you. What exactly did you find out in Abaddon about the curse?"

"Nothing," he said, belching. He'd managed to crawl over to the wall, snagging a bottle of tequila on the way, and was propped up, guzzling it.

"What do you mean nothing?" May asked, deftly whipping another bottle out of his reach when he tried to grab it off the table. "You've been there for a whole week. How can you have found out nothing?"

"Are you being dominant?" Magoth asked, slowly rising to his feet with a speculative glint in his eye.

"No," May said hastily, ignoring Gabriel when the latter growled softly. "Not in the way you like, anyway."

"I did not find out anything about the curse because there were no demons to question," Magoth said, lunging forward and managing to get ahold of the bottle before May could move away. "Asmodeus's halls were empty of all but a few wrath demons—who I could not question without making Asmodeus aware of the inquiry—an alchemist, and a mage in the dungeon."

"Where is everyone?" I asked no one in particular at the same time that May, with eyes narrowed in thought, asked, "Why would he empty his palace of his legions? Where did they go?"

"California," a female voice answered. "Vientiane. Seoul. Beijing. And oddly enough, São Paolo."

We turned en masse to see a woman who stood at the door. She smiled broadly at us, plopping down an oversized black-and-white striped canvas bag on the nearest chair before striding forward.

"Er ... this is a private gathering," Ysolde told her, looking as baffled as I felt. "But how do you know where the demons are?"

"And just who are you?" I asked. "I realize that sounds rude, but I warded that door to make sure no one could get through it unless they were dragonkin, and you don't look like a dragon to me."

"Are you with Asmodeus?" May asked, her fingers moving on the leather bustier she frequently wore. I knew she had at least one dagger hidden upon her person, and assumed it was tucked away there. "Has he sent you to do his bidding?"

"What is your business with dragonkin?" Drake asked with a bluntness that was borderline rude, moving forward to block the woman's view of me.

Instantly, Baltic and Gabriel mimicked the movement, hiding their mates from the intruder.

"We did not invite you to this meeting," Bastian said stiffly, moving next to Baltic. "You will explain your presence now."

"Or sooner," Kostya added, never one to be kept out of the game of scaring someone poop-less.

"Is there any more tequila?" Magoth was back at the libations table, ignoring us all as he poked around in a box that held various bottles.

"Wow," the woman said, her gaze moving along all of us. "You guys are, like, seriously scary. Except the demon lord. Although his penis has a hell of a curse."

"Pants!" May commanded to Magoth, who had indeed removed his leather trousers again. With a mean look at her, he put them on again before drinking half the bottle of tequila in one go.

I gave an exasperated mental roll of my eyes, and tucked my hand into the crook of Drake's arm as I moved to his side. "I think before anyone loses his temper, perhaps we ought to start over. Hi. I'm Aisling Grey, and this is my husband, Drake. And you are?"

"Sasha," she said, smiling happily at me. She had long brown hair that she wore in two flower-bedecked braids, a pair of hot pink tights, an orange denim miniskirt, and a blue-and-white striped off-the-shoulder top. She looked to be nineteen or twenty, and although nothing about her screamed Otherworld, she had to be someone extremely talented to get through the wards I'd used on the doors.

"Sasha what?" Kostya asked, looking suspicious as usual.

She tipped her head to the side as she looked at him, her smile fading. A sense of profound sadness seemed to leach out of her. "Just Sasha. Your friend is dead."

"Which friend?" Kostya asked quickly, taking a menacing step forward.

"The red dragon." Her gaze moved along us again, and settled on me. "All of them are dead. No, I tell a lie—three survived, but one is only a mate, so I'm not sure if she should be counted."

The next few minutes were filled with a whole bunch of angry dragons swarming the young woman named Sasha, pelting her with questions and demands for answers.

After a few minutes of that, I went to sit down, suddenly feeling tired.

"Are you all right?" May had detached herself from the others to crouch down next to me. "Are you feeling ill?"

"Yes, I'm fine, and no, not ill. Just tired of all the death."

"You believe her, then?" May asked, nodding toward where the dragons were towering over Sasha, clearly trying to intimidate her. Surprisingly, they weren't succeeding.

"Yes." I hesitated for a few seconds. "I don't quite know why, but I do."

May nodded. "As do I. I can't explain it, but I agree. Which means we have to get to the bottom of whatever it is she knows."

It took another fifteen minutes before peace was restored to the room. Magoth had been sent on his way, and the dragons had formally started the sárkány, recognizing Sasha as a special envoy to the meeting.

Drake started things off by saying, "You will tell us now why you say the red dragons are all dead. How did you come by this information?"

"All but three of the red dragons," Gabriel added. "Which three? How were the others killed?"

"And why?" Bastian questioned.

Sasha, seated across from me, looked around the table, then turned her attention back to me. "I have limited time here. There's so much for me to learn, you see, and I just started an apprenticeship with a very lonely man who is all the way on the West Coast of the US, so this is going to have to be quick. Your red dragon friend was killed saving his mate."

"Jian had a mate?" I shook my head, glancing at Drake. "Did we know this?"

"No." He looked thoughtful. "It must have happened recently."

"Very recent," Sasha confirmed. "The other red dragons were killed outright. What remains of the ones who had left the sept and were later taken ..." She glanced down at the table and shook her head. "They are no longer dragons."

All the wyverns spoke at once, but stopped when Drake held up a hand for silence. "How do you know this? Are you connected to the demons?"

"No. I'm an espirit. Or rather, I was one. Now I'm ..." She hesitated a few seconds, the corners of her mouth quirking. "I guess I'm just me. Sally said I needed to be out in the mortal world seeing what was going on, since she was wrapping up her own business. So I went to California, because as I said, I have work there. And then I figured it would be better for you guys to know what went down, since there was no one else to tell you what happened. So that's why I'm here. And yes," she said, looking directly at me. "I am extremely talented, although in weird ways. I can tie a knot in a cherry stem with my tongue. I can talk to birds, and I've seen sixty-seven total solar eclipses, which is pretty awesome if you think about it."

"Sally?" May glanced at Gabriel. "You know Sally?"

"I should. I'm taking over her job in"—she consulted her wrist, which would have been an innocuous gesture if she had been wearing a watch, but her wrist was bare of anything but a few freckles—"twenty-seven days, fifteen hours, and three minutes. Which is why I really have to be going. As I said, there's a man who I'm helping find his way out of the dark, so if you don't mind—"

She rose to a general clamor of voices demanding answers.

"Sorry, I'm just the messenger," Sasha said, popping on a pair of black-and-white polka-dot sunglasses and swinging the straps of her massive bag up onto her shoulder. "Oodles of warm fuzzies on the death of your friend and his family. Later, dragons!"

Before even the wyverns—who frequently moved so fast that they were just a blur—could react, she was gone, the soft click of the door closing behind her the only sound.

"Well," I said, slumping back in my chair, feeling as if I'd just been caught in a whirlwind. "That was a hell of a thing, wasn't it?"

"Jian's dead," Bastian said, shaking his head. "I understand what she said, but why? How?"

Drake looked blankly at nothing. I put my hand on his leg, just because I felt the need for the contact. Drake might hide his emotions from the other wyverns, but I knew he felt the loss of even members of other septs. "I couldn't say, but given that the rest of his sept was destroyed by demons, I assume he fell to them, as well."

"So much death," I said, feeling cold inside. "How many red dragons were lost in total? I didn't want to ask Jian that, since ... well, it was just rubbing salt in an open wound."

"I believe the number was in the low forties," Gabriel answered, glancing at Drake for confirmation.

The latter nodded. "That sounds right. About eighty or so left with Fiat after he killed Chuan Ren. They must have joined the tribe he formed with—" He stopped abruptly.

An uncomfortable silence fell over us until Bastian broke it.

"The tribe he formed when he rent the blue sept in two," he said, his voice filled with sadness. "That number sounds accurate to me, as well. Fiat has much to answer for, and not just to my sept."

"With all due respect to the loss of the red dragons, what do we do now?" Ysolde asked, scooting her chair a little closer to Baltic. "Are the demons going to pick off all the members of each sept? How do we fight them if so?"

Silence fell again. I stood up, saying when everyone looked at me, "Potty break. No one say anything interesting until I get back."

I hurried off to the bathroom and when I returned to the room rented for the sárkány, Drake was saying, "Let us examine what we know. Asmodeus is reported by a number of sources to be in the process of weaving a curse that will affect dragonkin. In addition, demons were used to kill or otherwise change the red dragons. By whom, or how, the latter was conducted is unclear."

"Jim and Magoth said that Abaddon is empty of Asmodeus's demons," I said, hurriedly taking my seat. "Which sounds to me like it's Asmodeus behind the whole shebang. Why is what gets me. How does he benefit from cursing and/or destroying dragons?"

"A curse would weaken us," Bastian said, gesturing the idea of it away. "It is not the curse that worries me."

"It may be that destruction is not necessarily Asmodeus's goal," Gabriel said slowly, one hand stroking along May's back.

"What do you mean?" she asked him, a frown furrowing her brow.

"Jian mentioned seeking a dragon hunter on the US West Coast. What if Asmodeus was attempting to—for the lack of another word, manufacture—an army of dragon hunters? Or rather, of antidragon hunters?"

"Oh, that's deep," I said, goose bumps rippling down my arms. "And devious. All the other demon lords would just have regular demons, but if Asmodeus filled his ranks with demons who also were dragons ..." I stopped, unable to continue at the horrible thought.

Drake nodded. "He would then be able to control not just all the other demon lords, but the mortal world, as well."

"So this is a play to gain control here, in our world?" Bastian said, suddenly looking furious. "He wishes to rule the dragonkin as well as the Otherworld?"

"It's the only thing that makes sense," I said slowly. "To be fair, it sounds like something Bael would do—he loved plans with layers like that—but since he's in the Akasha, it's entirely reasonable that Asmodeus would take a leaf out of Bael's playbook and go for global domination. I'll have to tell the Guardians' Guild. They will definitely want to know."

"How do we combat this plan to consume everyone?" Ysolde asked, her face tight with worry. I knew how she felt. The idea of the twins being sucked into Abaddon and turned into demonic soldiers made me want to run screaming from the room, collect up my babies, and hide them away somewhere safe.

"That we must stop Asmodeus before he proceeds any further goes without saying," Drake said, his fire hot inside him. I knew he was thinking of the children, as well. "I agree with Bastian that the curse—if there is one—is not as worrisome as having the septs fall to Asmodeus. It is he who must be stopped."

"Curses can be broken by Charmers," Bastian said, tapping the table. "Even one set by a demon lord. We must have Asmodeus's ring. The one that Kostya was supposed to find."

Everyone turned to look at Kostya, who scowled in return.

"I told you when you all decided it was my job to find it that I had no idea where to look for it! We don't even know for certain that it's in the mortal realm. Perhaps Asmodeus has it, and it is that which he is using to turn the red dragons."

Everyone chewed that thought over for a bit before Gabriel shook his head. "I think we would know if Asmodeus had the ring. It must be here. Which means we must find it."

"I hate to be the one in the slow lane when everyone else is zipping past me, but even if we find this magical Tolkien ring, how is that going to help? Can it stop Asmodeus from chomping up all the dragons and spitting them out in demon form?" I asked.

"Yes," all four wyverns said at the same time.

I slumped back in my chair. "Oh. Well, then, by all means, let's get it. It sounds like the answer to all our problems."

It took another half hour before it was decided that May and Gabriel would go ahead with their plan to approach Sally and seek her help in finding the mysterious ring, while Ysolde (much to Baltic's disgust) would try to pin down the First Dragon for, at the very least, information.

"And the rest of us?" I said as the others rose from their respective seats, the sárkány having been declared closed. "What do we do?"

Silence fell over us again for a few seconds while the wyverns all exchanged glances.

"Prepare," Drake said, and held out his hand for me.

I felt a distinctly ominous portent about the word that sent another skitter of goose bumps down my arms.

My dear Friia,

Are you aware of how difficult it is to locate, and influence, a minor demon in Abaddon?

Your devoted brother,
First Dragon

NINE

GROUP MAIL: MATES UNION MEMBERS

From: Aisling
Subject: Demons

My apologies for the e-mail, ladies, but it's faster for me to type on the laptop than use the voice-to-text on my phone. That thing is wildly inaccurate, and refuses to shut up when I tell it to, and then it blabs everything to Drake. Seriously, whoever made that function has a lot to answer for.

Where was I? Oh, the e-mail. So. After the sárkány, Drake and I talked about what we could do to help stop Asmo and his plan for the dragons, and naturally, I wanted to go fetch Jim, but he wouldn't let me, so I settled with texting Jim a few times. I tried to call, but it always seemed to have that pesky mage Helath with it. Regardless, here's what came out of the last exchange:

To: Jim

We need badly to know what Asmodeus is up to there. Have you heard anything about which dragon sept he's going to attack next?

From: Jim

What?

To: Jim

What dragon sept is Asmo going to target next? Oh god, it's us, isn't it? I'm going to have to tell Drake, and he'll go into super hyper fabu protective mode, and probably seal the twins and me up in an impenetrable vault somewhere deep in the base of an extinct volcano, and I'll end up having the baby on my own, without him there so I can tell him just what I think of him while I'm trying to push a small human out of a not-substantial opening. Damn that Asmodeus!

From: Jim

You're gonna have to cut back on your James Bond movies, 'cause you're starting to get them on the brain. Also, can you please not mention pushing your latest spawn out your hoohaw? It's almost dinnertime, and Helath's minion is making turkey chili with ghost peppers, and you know how I love me some spicy chili.

To: Jim

Just tell me the truth. I can take it.

From: Jim

About your hoohaw? I mean, I can give you a few general thoughts on the subject, although I haven't seen yours in particular, and can I say that I'm grateful about that? I loves ya big-time, Ash, but there are some things that just aren't right between a demon and its demon lord, and hoohaw-familiarity is one of those things.

To: Jim

Dammit, Jim! Stop talking about my private parts, which I was NOT asking you about. Tell me when Asmodeus is going to launch his next attack on us.

From: Jim

What attack?

To: Jim

The one you said he's going to make. Wait ... I guess you didn't say he was going to attack us. Is he? Going to attack the green dragons?

From: Jim

That would be a negative.

To: Jim

Really? I ... are you sure? Because it was pretty clear to us a couple of days ago when we had a sárkány, and it came out that all the red dragons were destroyed by Asmodeus.

From: Jim

Sometimes I worry about you. Like, shouldn't you know things by now? You've been a Guardian for a long time.

To: Jim

What have I missed? Dammit, Jim, don't make me command you in text, because I will.

From: Jim

Demons.

From: Jim

Specifically, Asmo's demons.

To: Jim

What about them?

From: Jim

There aren't any. I told you that, Ash. Man, don't tell me senility is hitting you now. I figured we'd have a few centuries before you went off to the land of the perpetually befuddled.

As you can imagine, ladies, at this point I was not only breathing heavily—a few teeth were being gnashed, as well. I include the texts just to show you why you should never summon a demon and bind it to yourself. Back to the drama that is my life with Jim …

To: Jim

Effrijim, I command thee to answer my questions with explicit details, starting with who Asmodeus is going to attack next.

From: Jim

You really were born to be a demon lord, you know that? You have that bossiness down pat. OK, OK, don't blow out your girdle. Asmodeus, to the best of my knowledge gleaned from the couple of peeps still left in his domain, is not attacking anyone. He can't. He has no demons left, his legions being depleted by Bael before he was banished to the Akasha, and then he used up a few more in creating the red dragon demons.

To: Jim

WHAT? He's not attacking us? And what do you mean he used up legions of demons? How could he use up demons unless he was making banes?

From: Jim

You think it's easy turning a dragon into demon-lite? It takes like almost a whole legion just to make one, and he made about sixty according to Helath, who was the one who figured out how to do it. He used a quintessence.

To: Jim

Holy cheese and guacamole! Are you sure? We need to be absolutely sure of this information.

From: Jim

Mostly sure. I can double-check if you are going to be pushy about it.

I told it to do that, and a couple of hours later, got the following:

From: Jim

Gotta make this quick because Asmo is in a rage over a spy he set on Bael, and the dude isn't responding. The demon, not Bael. Re: red dragons that weren't squashed into demon-hood–there aren't any. Demon reds killed them.

To: Jim

We know that. What about the fact that Asmodeus isn't planning on making more hybrids?

From: Jim

Like I said before, it takes a legion to do that, and Helath confirmed there just aren't any more of Asmo's legions left. GTG. Heard a rumor about a second spy that Asmo sent into the Akasha, and want to know if it's true or not.

To: Jim

Don't bother about Bael. He's out of our hair, and not likely to give us any grief. If there's nothing more you can do there, I'll send Magoth back in to fetch you. Just sit tight, and keep your head down. I don't want you getting hurt.

From: Jim

Smooches, babe.

So. There you have it. Drake is no doubt telling all the other wyverns what Jim reported, but I wanted to update you guys, since we all know how they—the men—can be annoying when they try to protect us by not spilling everything they know.

From: Ysolde

Subject: Wow. And also, how is your hoohaw?

That is an excellent report, Aisling. Thank you for providing it, and please pass on our collective thanks to Jim for doing such sterling undercover work in Abaddon. I'm more than a little flabbergasted to find out that Asmodeus used up his legions of demons making the red dragon demons, but it would explain why no other sept has reported attacks by demons. Dare we hope that it was a (horrible, and tragic beyond understanding) experiment that failed?

From: May

Subject: Thank the goddess. And I second concern about Aisling's nether bits. Is all well?

Gabriel just told me that Drake has, indeed, contacted the wyverns with the news Jim provided. Gabriel thinks it means we don't have to worry about the rest of us being turned into demons, but that we should find the couple of red dragons who Sasha said weren't affected or killed. We owe it to Jian to take care of his mate and the two other sept members. Poor woman. Poor red dragons.

From: Aisling

Subject: Concern appreciated, but not needed. Hoohaw is in fine form. So to speak.

Drake said much the same thing, May. He's asked a few green dragons who live in the US to go out to California in order to find Jian's mate. I feel awful about the whole situation with the red sept. That they should have been used for some horrible attempt by Asmodeus to control dragons is ... well, atrocious. Horrendous. Nightmare-making. My concern is that what he tried once, he may try again.

From: Ysolde

Subject: Happy to hear the good crotch news / also sad about red dragons

I agree. He's proved that he's a danger to the dragonkin. We have to take care of him. And yes, that means what you think—we need to find his ring, and bring him down. Or out. Do you bring a demon lord down from Abaddon, or out?

From: May

Subject: Abaddon nomenclature

You boot a demon lord out of Abaddon. Ask me how I know. #formerconsortproblems

From: Aisling

Subject: So glad you aren't married to Magoth anymore

May is absolutely correct, although it's not as easy as you might think, even though Bael, probably the most powerful demon lord there ever was, was banished to the Akasha. That took the combined Tools of Bael and Sally to accomplish, and much though I'd like to think Asmodeus's ring is akin to the One Ring, I doubt if it has the power to send him to the Akasha, too. Not without some serious intervention from a deity or two. Or maybe more artifacts of power.

From: May

Subject: Still have the tiny bit of leather and fluff Magoth made me wear at consort event (Gabriel loves it)

We'll talk to Sally. She might have some insight, since she is the one who handled the Bael banishing. Will report back when I have news.

My dear Friia,

What does a tiny violin have to do with my complaint about how difficult it is to influence demons in Abaddon? And just how tiny is the violin? I have always enjoyed music, but I cannot think that a violin that is classified as "tiny" would be agreeable to the ears.

Your devoted brother,
First Dragon

TEN

WANTED: MOVE-OUT CLEANER EXPERIENCED WITH STICKY SITUATIONS

Terrin was a man beset.

"Really, sugar, it's just too bad of you to keep involving yourself in things that don't concern the Court." Sally, with a dramatic gesture that didn't fool Terrin in the least, stormed past his desk, looking aggrieved. "First you insist we need a break because if we don't, all sorts of horrible things will happen to the world. Well, to be fair, that's not the worst idea—the vacation, not the horrible things—because we've been at this for so long without any sort of time off."

"You were a demon lord," Terrin reminded her. "I would qualify you flitting around Abaddon as time off. Whereas I had to remain here and keep the Court running."

"Only because you insist on being a steward," Sally said, marching past his desk with another dramatic gesture. "Then you make me help May and her truly magnificent dragon, which, I will admit, also wasn't too terrible. But still. The fact remains that you keep dipping your fingers into pies that aren't by rights ours."

"I find it hard to allow people to suffer when a little nudge in the right direction can help things along," Terrin said with perfect equanimity. Sally might bluster and storm about, but he knew her well, and although she liked to put up a show about helping mortals and immortals alike, she had almost as soft a heart as he did.

"Yes, but that's not our job. We're here to monitor the Court, not what goes on outside of it."

Terrin shrugged, and flipped over the next report that was waiting for him to review. He scanned through the data, saying absently, "We *are* supposed to be the good guys."

"There's good, and then there's good," Sally said with a mild sniff of annoyance, and Terrin knew she'd go on for approximately eight more minutes until she ran out of steam, but before she could continue, a low-level clerk tapped on the door to Terrin's small office, and popped his head around the door.

"You have visitors. You want to see them here, or out in the square?"

Terrin gestured toward the large stack of paperwork filling his in tray. "I can't leave until I get through this, so bring whoever it is here."

"And that's another thing," Sally said, stalking over to the window to look out at the small square that bustled with the beings of the Court of Divine Blood, which was currently in the form of a quasi-medieval village, complete with central square and Disneyesque castle.

He'd left the choice of this appearance of the Court to Sally, and she'd allowed her inner Mad King Ludwig run wild.

"What is?" he asked, moving on to the next item in his stack.

"This work you insist on doing. You're always at it. You could delegate, you know. We could get a proper steward in."

"I like to feel useful," he protested, glancing up at her. "My midlevel management skills are what you said you loved best about me."

"And it is, darling, of course it is," Sally answered, waving a hand again. "But there has to be more to life than just shuffling—gracious! What are you two doing here?"

The last words were spoken to the people who entered the room, a slight woman with a 1920s bobbed haircut, and a tall man with a short goatee and the most silver eyes he'd ever seen on a man.

But of course, he wasn't a man. This had to be Sally's May and Gabriel.

"Sally!" May said, looking surprised as she glanced between her and Terrin. "I—we were told that you were gone, and that we'd have to talk to your … er …" She gestured toward Terrin.

"Partner," he said, and, standing up, shook first May's hand, then Gabriel's. "At least I will be for a few more days until our replacement comes in."

"I'm not here, not really," Sally said, giving Terrin a long look. "I just popped in to read Terrin the riot act, and then I'm off. Sweetness, I assume you are duly chastised?"

"Not in the least," he told her, aware of the glint of humor in her eye. He had a feeling that he was about to be left holding the bag, however, and he watched Sally for a moment to see if she was expecting him to do her dirty work, or if she was leaving matters up to his judgment.

"I'm so glad we found you," May said, turning to Sally. "We really need your help—"

"I'm sure you do, sugar, but as I've told you before, the Carrie Fay Academy of Perky Bosoms and Truly Magnificent Hair helps those who help themselves, so I'm afraid it's to them you will have to turn in this, your time of beauty needs. Farewell, my lovelies!"

The glance Sally slipped him when she blew a kiss to him told Terrin exactly what he wanted to know. He sighed and, with a regretful look at the stack of papers that he told himself he'd get through before he could leave the Court in Sasha's hands, resigned himself to the inevitable.

"Sally, wait—well, dammit!" May said, following her to the door. "She's disappeared. That's just mean of her. She knows full well we need help, and she bailed on us. Flat out bailed on us. Is there some sort of quality-control people I can complain to? Because I'll leave her a hell of a review—"

May stopped, obviously remembering where she was.

Terrin smiled. "Unfortunately, Sally travels to the beat of her own drummer. I'm afraid there's little anyone can do to remedy that. Now, if you don't mind, I have a great deal of work awaiting me before the transition of service can be made. . . ." He let the sentence trail off with obvious meaning.

The silver wyvern shared a look with the doppelganger before they both turned to him. "Naturally, we understand that you have a great many pressing matters," Gabriel said, sliding an arm around his mate. "We do not wish to interrupt your work, but we—the dragonkin—were made aware of a grave situation by Sally, and we seek further information regarding that."

"Grave situation?" He leaned back in his chair, his fingertips together as he considered first the dragon, then his mate. "You refer to the situation with a curse originating in Abaddon?"

"Yes." Gabriel, at Terrin's nod, pulled up a couple of chairs, and the pair sat, their expressions tight with worry. "Sally came to us with the former demon lord Magoth, and informed us we needed to investigate the situation in Abaddon. The information we have just had from there is confusing at best, but it drives home the point that it behooves the dragonkin to take into our possession the ring that is said to have once belonged to Asmodeus."

"Indeed," Terrin said, considering the matter for a handful of seconds. "That would seem to be wise."

"That's where we want Sally to help us," May said, leaning forward to pin him back with a gaze that in any other being he would say was aggressive. He was amused that this little doppelganger had such a fiery spirit, then decided it was only fitting for her role as a wyvern's mate. "No one knows where this ring is. Or even if it really exists."

"Oh, it exists," Terrin said, wondering how far the dragons would go in an attempt to destroy Asmodeus. He had a feeling that if they were to band together, they might just achieve such an impressive feat.

"It does?" May shot Gabriel a glance and sat back, obviously relieved. "Good, because we desperately need it. Or at least borrow it for a bit. Where is it?"

"Of that, I could not tell you," Terrin said, easing a stapled report about the interaction between cherubs and mortals from the stack, and giving it a longing look.

"You can't?" May looked disappointed. "But ... you're the Sovereign."

"One-half of the Sovereign," he corrected, initialing a funds-transfer request. "And much though mortals believe otherwise, omnipotence does not come attached with the job."

"What is the use in being the Sovereign—sorry, one-half of the Sovereign—if you don't know how to help people?" May said with a decided edge to her voice.

Gabriel, with an amused look at her, gave a polite cough. "I think, little bird, we should not be so hasty to assume that Terrin is unable to help us."

"He just said he doesn't know where the ring is," May said, her expression disgruntled.

"But he did not say he wouldn't help us locate it," Gabriel told her with a quirk of his lips.

Terrin sighed for a third time, decided he had to nip that particular habit in the bud, and tapped a few times on the keyboard that sat before him. "As it happens, you are both correct. It would make my job infinitely easier if I were omnipotent, and also, I am willing to help you. Or rather, since my hours here are dwindling, I am happy to put you in contact with one who can help you."

"We would be grateful for any assistance in this matter," Gabriel said in a formal manner that Terrin knew dragons adopted with those beings outside their septs.

Terrin picked up a pencil and rustled through the stack of paper until he found a pad of paper bearing the name and motto of a company that specialized in the removal of poltergeists' extraneous appendages, and asked, "If you would give me your phone numbers?"

They did so, and although it was clear that neither of them wanted to leave without getting information about how and where they could find Asmodeus's ring, Terrin managed to escort them to the courtyard without more than a few pointed looks by the doppelganger.

* * *

To: Sally, Sasha

Really, my dear, you could have dealt with that yourself rather than running off. The wyvern and his mate were perfectly reasonable people, even when it was clear they would have preferred that I give them Sasha's information rather than wait to speak with you both.

From: Sally

But you deal with people so much better than I do! Plus, I already did my good deed. You said when I did that all would be set into motion, and I could go to the Maldives with a clear conscience.

From: Sasha

I thought you were going to Fiji? Also, what good deed did you do? Asking for a friend. #maybeinslightamountofhotwater

To: Sally, Sasha

Slight amount? Er ...

From: Sally

Oh no. You didn't. I told you not to. Tell me you didn't. Please, tell me you didn't.

To: Sally, Sasha

Eh? What's going on?

From: Sasha

Yeah, as to that ... it seemed like the thing to do even though you said I shouldn't get involved.

From: Sasha

I am an apprentice, after all. You wanted me to

learn all the jobs, so I'm learning how to be a dragon hunter. Plus, we're benevolent and all that crap.

From: Sally

For the love of the twelve hours and eighteen tiny little saints ... Terrin, would you please inform our replacement why it is not a good idea for her to interfere with situations that others need to conquer in order to prosper?

To: Sasha, Sally

What happened? What did Sasha do? Did she smite some demons? If so, I can hardly blame her for that. I used to love smiting demons way back in the days before we signed that agreement with Abaddon.

From: Sasha

Not smiting. It was ... there was an incident with a dragon hunter.

From: Sally

Incident? What sort of incident?

From: Sasha

Well ... maybe I better not say.

To: Sally, Sasha

Oh, dear. That bad?

From: Sally

I want it recorded that I told her not to get involved. Not to such an extent that there are "incidents."

From: Sasha

I think everything will turn out all right. Probably. Possibly. It depends on a couple of people, but I'm mostly almost sure it will be OK.

To: Sasha, Sally

Sally, is there room on your flight to the Maldives? I begin to believe I might leave earlier than I had originally planned.

From: Sasha

Oh, come on. It's my job to help peeps! I'm helping peeps!

From: Sally

You don't do the work for them, Sasha. You give them the help they need to make their own choices and work toward their own goals.

To: Sally, Sasha

I'm afraid she's right, my dear. We may meddle now and again, but we strive to keep our assistance limited in such ways that those involved can choose to take whatever actions they like regardless of our interactions.

From: Sasha

Great. I'm in hot water before I even get started. What do I need to do to fix things?

From: Sally

With regards to the dragon hunter incident? Only you can say.

From: Sasha

Don't worry, I'll make things right. I think. As I said, it kind of depends on a couple of other people, but I'm pretty sure that Ian is on board. Or he will be once he gets back from Abaddon. Is there something I can do to help you, Terrin? Some filing? Some benevolent act? Fetch a latte or two?

To: Sally, Sasha

Are you asking because you feel guilty, or because you know Sally is going to lecture you within an inch of your life the minute she gets you alone?

From: Sally

Darlin', you know me so well.

From: Sasha

Both. Mostly because I feel bad that you're trying

to get everything in good order before I officially take charge.

To: Sally, Sasha

As it happens, there is a situation that I hoped you would be able to help with. It appears that Asmodeus is in search of his ring, and it needs to be secured somewhere safe.

From: Sally

Terrin!

To: Sally, Sasha

Hmm?

From: Sally

You're almost as naughty as I am!

To: Sally, Sasha

But not quite, I think. Besides, it's just a temporary situation.

From: Sally

True, but you know that's not what the dragons want.

To: Sally, Sasha

Ah, but it's what they need, and that, I think, is of greater importance.

From: Sasha

Preach it, brother!

From: Sally

Ahem.

From: Sasha

Whoops. Nothing to see here. Move along. ...

To: Gabriel, May, Sasha

Gabriel and May, I would like to introduce you to Sasha. She is taking over at the Court of Divine Blood in a short time, and has offered to help with the item we discussed.

From: May

Sasha? The Sasha who came to our sárkány and told us Jian was dead? That Sasha?

From: Sasha

Hi again!

From: May

Hello. Er ... you have Asmodeus's ring? Or you know where it is?

From: Sasha

Neither, but I might know someone who knows someone who may have seen it a few years ago. Sit tight. I'll get to work on it.

From: Gabriel

Thank you, Sasha and Terrin. May and I, as well as the rest of the dragonkin, greatly appreciate your help.

From: Sasha

No prob!

My dear Friia,

Do you have any reach into the Court of Divine Blood? The Sovereign is being annoying by refusing to respond to my requests, despite a most desperate need for a particular Charmer to be found.

Your devoted brother,
First Dragon

ELEVEN

ENTER BEE, STAGE LEFT

“Hmm.”

“Hmm?”

I looked at the address displayed in the text message.

From: Court of Divine Blood

Bee Dakar: take the entrance at 15 Elizabeth Place, Islington. I’ll be on the other side at 1pm.

Slowly, I answered the man who waited impatiently. “Hmm, as in this doesn’t look at all like heaven.”

The driver gave me an odd look as I climbed out of his car while simultaneously tapping on the rideshare app. “It’s a chip shop, mate. It may look like heaven, but it’s a vector of heart disease and clogged arteries. Take my advice and stay away from it.”

“Yes, I know what it is, but it’s also … oh, never mind. This is the right address. Thanks for the pickup.”

The man gave me one last dubious look, but his phone pinged at that moment, indicating the tip I’d just given, so he drove off without further comments disparaging either the fish-and-chip shop (which I agreed had a patina of cholesterol hanging over its head like a saturated death cloud) or me. I took a deep breath, immediately coughing on the petrol belched out by a nearby lorry. "London," I muttered under my breath. "Not my favorite place in the world. Give me the South of France any day."

The chip shop smelled as bad as I thought it would, but luckily, a door on a side wall led to an inner passage. The shop employees, no doubt influenced by the same spell that hid the door to those of a mortal persuasion, ignored me when I hurried past a line of laconic teens, and scruffy-haired men holding racing forms.

"This had better be important, that's all I'm saying," I continued to complain when I hurried through a deep purple swirling miasma that was the entrance to the Court of Divine Blood. "I'm burning up my vacation time as is, and—oh. Hello."

A young woman of about nineteen or twenty sat on the end of a waist-high stone wall that lined a stretch of velvety green grass. Ahead of us, a massive stone building resembling a Disney artist's idea of a European castle rose, complete with blue tiled roof, spiky turrets, and occasional pennant flags waving lazily in the breeze.

"There you are! You're Bee, aren't you? I like the name. Are you really a Beatrice?"

"No, I'm just Bee. My parents had a thing for honeybees. You're … er …" I consulted the e-mail on my phone. "Sorry, there's no name."

"I'm Sasha," she said with a friendly smile.

"Pleasure to meet you. I understand you need something charmed."

"Likewise." She hopped down off the wall, giving me a sunny smile that I felt to my toes. There was something odd about her, something that warned me that she might look like she just left an anime cosplay convention, but in reality, there was a whole lot more to her. "And no, I don't need anything charmed, but I do have a job for you. I'd like you to fetch a ring for me."

"A ring?" I frowned, falling into place alongside her when she marched past the castle, toward a long, low building to the side. "What sort of ring?"

"Unicorn, I think." She paused for a moment and thought, then gave a shrug. "You'll have to ask Ysabelle that. She'd know."

"Ysabelle? Belle Raleigh? You know Belle?"

"Nope. But you do. You lived with her, right?"

"When I was in college, yes. Is this … uh … a stable?" I asked when I had to sidestep a large mound of manure. The low building appeared at odds from the rest of the area that mortals thought of as heaven, but really was just an eclectic collection of people who worked for an entity known as the Sovereign.

"It is. There's a litter of kittens in the back stall. I've told Sally that I have dibs on the stripy one, but now I'm thinking the ginger is more adorable."

Feeling more than a little confused, I followed her into the stable, blinking at the darkness within. The air inside was close, but unlike mortal stables, it was not filled with the scent of rodent droppings. This one smelled of hay warmed under a summer sun, and sleepy horses, contrasting pleasantly with the slightest overtone of saddle soap. I duly admired the barn cat's babies, trying to think how best to proceed.

"You're a friend of Sally, I assume," I said with studied nonchalance. Not everyone knew that the current

Sovereign was really two people who shared the job, and I didn't want to spill any beans if Sasha was one of the uninformed.

"You could say that." She held a kitten in each hand, and rubbed them gently against her cheeks. "I'm their underpinning."

I stared at her, even more confused. "You're what?"

She paused in the act of kitten-rubbing to scrunch up her nose in an adorable manner that I knew I would never in a million years be able to pull off. "That's not right? Underpants? No … ah! Understudy. That's the word. I'm taking over for them."

"Hell's bells! You're going to be the next Sovereign?"

"Yuppers. Do you like the ginger one or the gray tabby best?" she asked, holding out the kittens. "Sally said I could only have one, since the rest are spoken for, but I think I should be allowed to have two. That way they won't get lonely when I'm away helping out mortals."

"I like both, and I didn't know that the Sovereign helped mortals. I thought they just handled Court issues," I said slowly, trying to pick through what I knew about the setup in the Court of Divine Blood. It wasn't a lot, although I had met Sally a few years back.

"Good. I'll take both. It's only humane, right?" She returned the kittens to their sleepy mama, and rose, making herding gestures with her hands. "Welp, gotta run! People to pester, a sword to reclaim from the most adorable dragon hunter you ever did see, and a couple of sisters to round up, because you just know they're going to be needed in the end. Or maybe the middle." She thought for a minute, then nodded. "Yes, definitely the middle. The end is going to be something no one expects."

"The end of what?" I couldn't help but ask even though I was starting to realize that Sasha was not someone who provided answers to all the questions she generated.

"Exactly! That's what I've been saying all along," she answered, just like that made any sort of sense.

"OK, I'm done trying to understand what you're talking about." I allowed myself to be shooed out of the stable. "Let's focus on what's important. What ring, and what does it have to do with Belle, and while we're doing question and nonanswer period, why do you need a Charmer to fetch a ring?"

"Didn't I tell you?" She slapped on a huge Scarlett-O'Hara-at-a-barbecue hat, and grinned. "It's karma. You need it. No. Wait." She paused and narrowed her eyes for a moment, staring at nothing in particular. "I tell a like."

"Lie."

"Really?"

"Yes. The phrase is 'I tell a lie.' What I find curious is why someone who is the Sovereign's understudy doesn't know colloquial English."

Her grin grew. "I've been away for a while. What was I saying? Oh, I tell a lie. You don't need it now, but you will need it later. Karma, that is, not the ring, although the ring would probably like you, but you shouldn't use it without protection. So go forth and do your good deed and get the ring from Ysabelle. Just be sure you give it to someone really pure of heart, because you absolutely don't want it getting in the wrong hands."

"Wait, what?" I stopped and tried to grab Sasha as she scurried past me, a gigantic bag slung over one shoulder, but she just gave a little ripple of laughter and danced off, her long hair streaming after her. "Hang on! I'm supposed to what? I thought you wanted the ring?"

"Oh no, I can't have it," she called back, waving at me as she disappeared around a corner of the Disney castle. "That would violate any number of treaties. Hasta la vista, baby!"

"How do you know Terminator quotes, but you don't know 'I tell a lie'? That's all shades of wrong!" I yelled after her, but the only response I got was the faintest hint of laughter riding the wind.

"Dammit," I swore, then looked around guiltily in case any of the denizens of heaven heard me swear in their august domain. "Now what am I supposed to do?"

The answer, such as it was, came two days later. It took me that long to track down where Belle had gone to live.

"What are you doing in Vienna?" I asked my old friend after surprising her by showing up on her doorstep early one morning. "I thought the man you married was French?"

"He is, but he's also a Dark One, and helps with the Moravian Council," she answered, pouring out coffee and offering me a selection of breakfast pastry. "So we stay in Austria for part of the year, and the other part we live in England. Boys, if you are going to roughhouse, please go to the playroom. Bee has come a very long way to see me, and she doesn't want to be drowned out by your wrestling."

Two towheaded boys of nine and seven, both with startlingly blue eyes, emerged from where they had been rolling around behind the couch, and bearing innocent expressions that I didn't for a minute believe. "But, Mum," the younger boy said, reluctantly getting to his feet at Belle's gesture. "Chris and I are playing alchemist and heretic. We can't do that without fighting."

"You most certainly can. Why don't you two go to the library and entertain yourselves there?"

"We can't," Christian said, giving his brother a swift kick to the shins. "Roland annoyed Papa by trying to bespell him, and he banished us while he was working."

I stifled the urge to giggle both at the martyred look on Belle's face and at the two boys, who immediately broke into a scuffle when Roland objected to be kicked for what he claimed was no reason.

"Then go to your room," she told the boys, grabbing each one by a respective ear and hustling them toward the door.

"But there's nothing to do there," whined Roland.

"You may play Fortnight for one half hour. But not a minute more until you've finished your lessons, mind," she warned the boys, who promptly whooped with joy and thundered out of the room and up the stairs.

"If you weren't such a natural at being a mum, I'd offer you sympathy for those two hell spawns of yours," I said, accepting one of the pastries, even though I knew it would go straight to my hips. "They are adorable children, nonetheless. How is Sebastian?"

"Handsome as ever," Belle said with a happy sigh, then gave a little laugh. "That sounds so shallow, doesn't it? Truly, he is fine. Devoted to the boys and me, of course, but busy right now with some rumors of a long-lost threat to the Moravians."

"Really? What sort of a threat? No, wait, forget I asked that," I said, holding up a hand when I glanced at a clock on the mantel. "There's nothing more that I'd rather do than have a good, long catch-up chat with you, but I'm on a tight schedule. Do you know a young woman named Sasha?"

"Sasha?" Belle looked thoughtful, rolling the name around on her tongue. "Hmm. I don't think so. Is it someone from my past? You know how bad I am with names."

Given that Belle's past extended back more than five hundred years, she couldn't be blamed for forgetting a few names. "I couldn't say, although I can't help but feel if you've ever met Sasha, you'd remember her." I gave her a quick description of my visit to the Court of Divine Blood, ending with, "And that's why I showed up unannounced on your doorstep this morning."

"You're always welcome, of course," she said absently, obviously deep in thought. "I had no idea that the Court was undergoing another renaissance, which they must be if this Sasha person is taking over as Sovereign. How very interesting. I will have to tell Sebastian, in case it has some bearing on the Moravian Council."

"Do vampires often have dealings with the Court?" I asked, distracted by that thought.

She gave a delicate shrug. "Not normally, but you never know. Of late, things have felt a bit ..."

I waited for her to finish the sentence, but she said nothing more, just looked troubled.

"If there is a problem giving me the ring that Sasha mentioned—" I started to say, feeling more and more uncomfortable about the job that I'd reluctantly accepted. "I will totally understand if you don't feel like you can hand it over. After all, I'm a Charmer, not a courier or even someone with your experience concerning magical items."

She made a face, then gave a little chuckle. "There is something to be said for having an alchemist for a father. No, I have no problem with giving you the ring. You're welcome to it. Sebastian has wanted me to get rid of it for years, and with the boys into everything these days … no, the trouble doesn't lie with the ring." She looked up from where she'd been studying her hands, and seemed to pierce me with her straightforward gaze. "I'm just worried by the confluence of a number of situations. First, there are hints that the old threat to Moravians has returned. Then, rumors are swirling around about a massive number of demons being seen around the world, and finally, one of my friends who is mated to a dragon tells me the septs are closing ranks against some major event. It just feels as if the world is on the edge of a precipice, and I don't like the feeling at all."

"I wish I had something to say to make you feel better, but I'm afraid all I know is what Sasha told me, and precious little that was," I said, feeling helpless, just as if I were a tiny leaf afloat on a swollen river.

"It doesn't matter," Belle said with a shake of her head. Then she pulled on a gold chain hanging around her neck, and slipped it over her head. Dangling on the end of it was a simple gold-and-cream ring. It didn't look at all like anything of value, and yet as I accepted it, a slight tremor in the ring warned that it was just as aware of me as I was of it. "When the head of heaven tells you to do something, it behooves you to do it. Take the ring with my blessing. Who will you give it to?"

"There's really only one person who I'd trust with something so powerful," I said, eyeing the ring where it swung from the end of the chain. Before I could lose my nerve, I slipped the chain over my head and tucked the ring away into the valley between my breasts.

"Your brother?" Belle asked, surprising me.

"Rowan? No. Not that I wouldn't trust him with anything, up to and including my life, but he is too caught up in his own situation to cope with any more responsibility." I stood up, giving Belle a swift kiss on either cheek in parting. "No, this is going to have to go right back to the Court."

"But . . . you said Sasha wouldn't take it," Belle said, escorting me to the front door.

"Because she's going to be Sovereign," I said with a smile. "But if she's Sovereign, that means Sally is fair game."

"Ah," Belle said, her smile matching mine. "Smart thinking. Godspeed, Bee Dakar. Come back when you have time for a visit. Sebastian and the boys will be delighted to have you stay with us."

"Just as soon as I can clear my calendar, I'm all yours," I promised, and with a swift hug hurried off to the airport.

Six hours later, I passed through the portal from the London chip shop to the Court of Divine Blood and, after seeking help from a passing bureaucrat, found myself in a small office block disguised as one of the Disney castle's outbuildings.

As I entered the office I was assured was Sally's home when she was present, I found a man with brown hair and eyes, and a slightly aggrieved manner, hunched over a laptop, muttering curses in Latin under his breath.

"Oh," I said, coming to an abrupt halt, then glancing around just as if I'd find Sally hiding in a corner. "I'm so sorry, I must have the wrong office. I was looking for Sally—"

"You couldn't be any more sorry than I am," the man said, sighing and tapping on the laptop's keyboard a couple more times. "I don't suppose you know how to break an encrypted password?"

"I'm afraid not. Er ... can you tell me how to find Sally's office, please? I wouldn't bother you, but this is of great importance, and I'm in a bit of a hurry ..."

"Everyone is in a hurry these days," he said, pushing away the laptop and slumping back in the chair, one hand rifling his hair. "This is Sally's office, for what it's worth. It's her password I'm trying to ascertain, because of course she went jetting off without leaving it, and how she expects me to finish up all her work is beyond me."

"That must be difficult," I said, the penny dropping. This was obviously Sally's secretary. Or assistant. Or whatever the head of the Court had as an aide. "My name is Bee. I was hoping to leave something with Sally."

"You can put it in the box," the man said, gesturing toward a half-filled wooden crate, obviously used to gather up the last of Sally's office possessions. I eyed it, and then studied the assistant for a moment. He looked like a very nice, normal, innocuous man. He reminded me of my dentist, a man of quiet habits and very clean hands.

"I'm not sure. ... Is she going to be back here soon?"

He looked thoughtful for a moment, then shrugged. "I'd say no, but with Sally, you're never quite certain. Did you need her for anything in particular?"

"In a way, yes, but maybe you can pinch-hit," I said. "I have something that needs to go to Sally. Something very important, and not to be offensive, it really does need to go to the right person. Namely, Sally."

He looked at the chain with the ring swinging from it as I pulled it off and held it out. His shoulders slumped a bit. "That is ... I was not quite expecting this. I thought for certain that ... but that's neither here nor there, I suppose. You are aware that what you hold is Asmodeus's signet, yes?"

"Yes." I gave the ring a little frown. "It makes me kind of nervous, to be honest."

"And you wish to give Sally the ring? Please be aware that your verbal agreement is legally binding."

"Oh, you're recording me? Are you ... er ... I hate to be rude, but you're authorized to take important artifacts for her?"

"I am," he said with a smile that seemed to bathe me in warmth and comfort.

I was about to demand that at the very least I talk to Sally, but at his smile I felt remarkably confident that he was trustworthy. "Very well." I cleared my throat. "I, Bee Dakar, do willingly and of my own free will hand this ring, once belonging to the demon lord Asmodeus, to Sally, one-half of the Sovereign of the Court of Divine Blood."

"Former," the clerk said, tapping on his laptop.

"Sorry, yes, formerly one-half of the Sovereign. Will that do?"

"It will," he said with another reassuring smile, and, to my utter relief, took the ring and placed it into a small wooden box he'd extracted from a desk drawer. "I hope there is nothing more you need, because I really am behind, and must get things wrapped up by midnight."

One part of my brain warned that he was behaving somewhat cavalier about a ring that I had heard bore great power, but looking deep into his eyes, I saw nothing that made me doubt my actions. "I don't want to seem overly dramatic, but I feel obligated to remind you that the ring will need to be protected. Sasha seemed quite insistent about that."

"And so it will be," he answered, closing the laptop, and with another sigh slipped it into a leather satchel before glancing around the room. I realized then just how empty the office was, stripped bare of all items that might normally be found therein.

"You'll tell Sally to put it away somewhere safe?" I asked, even though I felt like I was being overly cautious. "Somewhere really safe?"

His expression was one of martyrdom. "Yes, it will be safe. I believe the opportunity to send it to a very safe place indeed will be presenting itself shortly, so you may rest assured that it will be kept secure until you have need of it later. And now, if you will excuse me, I must see the seneschal about clearing out Sally's personal rooms. She left a great deal of equipment that would be far better suited to Abaddon than the Court, and I'd prefer getting such devices out before anyone can see them."

"Thank you so much," I called after the odd little clerk as he left. I stood for a few minutes, troubled by something he'd said, murmuring aloud to the now-empty room. "Until I have need of it later? Now, just what in the wide, wide world of weird does that mean?"

My dear Friia,

I read your "family newsletter" with interest. You are indeed lucky to have so many of your firstborn surviving still, and active in your life. All but one of mine have perished over the centuries. The path of the firstborn was not an easy one to tread while they fought to control their fiery natures.

I recently came across one of the second-born. Comparing him to your grandchildren, I realized that there is much to be said about not giving your kin too much free rein.

Your devoted brother,
First Dragon

TWELVE

CONSTANTINE COMES TO A FEW HARD TRUTHS

"Please don't go. It's dangerous." Ysolde's voice had a pleading note to it.

Constantine threw himself at her feet. "My beauteous one! That you care so much warms my heart like—"

"Get up, you ass. She's speaking to me, not you." Baltic, ever the fly in Constantine's aphrodisiac ointment, strode through his admittedly noncorporeal form, and clasped his beloved Ysolde, kissing her soundly. "You fret unduly, *chérie*. It will take us less than half a day to go to Saint Petersburg and return."

"But the red dragon demons—" Ysolde started to protest, her lovely eyes shadowed.

Constantine, with a sigh at the fact that her eyes were never so shaded when she looked at him, rose and dusted himself off, even though no dirt could cling to his spirit form. "Were I your mate, I would never leave your side," he announced.

"They will not harm us," Baltic said, kissing her again. "Pavel and I have not existed as long as we have to be taken unawares by a couple of demons."

"And yet," Constantine said, buffing a nail and examining it as he spoke, "I could have sworn that you were resurrected only some forty years before. Forty years is nothing when compared to the long life some of us have lived."

Baltic glared at him. "Given that my mate raised you just a year ago, you have no grounds to cast stones. In fact, you shouldn't be here at all. Begone, pesky spirit, and leave Ysolde to rest as she should since she is still recovering from the trauma of birthing my son."

Constantine heard a distinct giggling in Ysolde's region, but her expression was placid as she gazed upon the annoying Baltic, one hand on his chest.

"If you are gone, then I will remain in the mortal world to keep Ysolde company and watch over her safety," Constantine said stiffly.

"And what do you plan to do should an attacker arrive?" Baltic asked with what Constantine thought was a particularly obnoxious tone. "Annoy them to death?"

"I am wyvern of the silver dragons," Constantine said, straightening his shoulders. "And I can adopt a physical presence, as you well know."

"You *were* wyvern, but you are nothing now but a blight on our existence. No, Ysolde, do not speak that reprimand I see trembling on your lips. I have not the time to teach this ghost yet again that he is here only because you begged me to allow him to remain. We must leave now if we are to make our flight. We will attend to the business meeting, and be back for supper."

"I just worry about you being out in public," Ysolde said, trailing after Baltic and his lieutenant Pavel, her voice plaintive. "Everything we've heard about the red dragons says they are very dangerous."

"You worry unduly," Baltic told her, and, to Constantine's disgust, gave her yet another lengthy kiss. Really, did the man have no sense of propriety? How many times did he feel it necessary to molest the glorious Ysolde with his lips?

"Farewell, my love," she said, standing at the door and waving as the two men got into a car. "Do not take any chances! I could not live should anything happen to—oh thank the goddess, they're finally gone."

Ysolde spun around and almost ran right through Constantine, so quickly did she move, the door slamming shut behind her.

"My beauteous one?" Constantine asked, somewhat startled. Was this the moment that he had hoped and dreamed about his entire life? Well, most of his life.

He thought for a second, and mentally corrected the statement to the few years he had lived after meeting Ysolde, and the time since she had resurrected him.

He cleared his throat. "You have come to your senses at last? I admit that you have taken me aback, although I am naturally on my knees with gratitude that you have done so."

He would have suited action to word, but Ysolde, without a glance at him, strode off into a small library that she had claimed as her own, muttering to herself as she did so.

"Ysolde?" Constantine followed after her slowly, unsure of what she wished of him, still more than a little scandalized that she could be at the door professing her undying love to the bastard Baltic, and then all but throw herself into his arms.

Could it be that he misread her?

"Is he awake?" he heard Ysolde ask via a small device that the boy Brom had told him was a baby monitor. "He just fed a half hour ago, but if he's awake, then I'll come upstairs—"

"No, he's asleep," the female green dragon whom Baltic had engaged as nursery help answered. Constantine was disappointed in the woman chosen, since she was happily mated to Brom's tutor. "We're fine here. I'll put in some time on my psychology-class homework while you get your chores done."

"Perfect, Raven. I just need an hour or so, but if Anduin wants feeding before that, let me know."

Constantine frowned at that. She expected him to seduce her in just an hour? "My glorious one, I am happy to oblige you, naturally, but there is such a thing as rushing through pleasurable events that can be enjoyed to their fullest with more care and detail—"

Ysolde looked up from where she was pulling out one desk drawer after another, frowning when she saw him. "Oh, Constantine, did you want something? I'm busy."

That most definitely did not sound as if she wished to have an assignation with him. He cherished the sensation of wounded ego, ignoring the part of his brain that had been surprised that she was finally acceding to his persistent wooing, and was now sighing in relief that he wouldn't be called to put into action all those claims of undying love. "Eh?" he asked, feeling more than a little adrift, conversationally speaking.

"I've got some things to do before Baltic gets back, and can't stop to chat with you, so if you don't mind finding something else to do, I'd be grateful," she answered, pulling out the bottommost drawer on the small desk she used for her laptop. "Brom and Nico should be out in the forensic shed, if you wanted to help them dissect a dead crow that Brom found the other day. Where is it? I pulled it out of Baltic's lair so I'd have it, but now I can't remember which drawer I put it in..." The last sentences were clearly spoken aloud to herself.

"Much as I would like to spend time with the son who Baltic did not sire, it is your presence that draws me like a moth to flame," he said, feeling the poetic turn of phrase demanded a bow and a suitably dramatic kiss to her delicate hand. Accordingly, he pulled on his energy to make himself corporeal, then made his best court bow.

Unfortunately, just as he did so, she exclaimed, "Oh, it's here!" and bent to open another drawer, resulting in their heads clunking together.

"Ow! Constantine!" She rubbed her forehead. "I just told you that I'm busy. Don't you have something else to do but get in my way?"

Her words cut him to the quick, but the sun would never rise on a day when he would criticize his beloved former (even if it was only for a few hours) mate. He bowed again, stiffly this time. "I live, as ever, to please you, and if you wish me to be gone, then I shall do so."

She narrowed her eyes on him. "Actually, now that I think about it, maybe you can help me."

His mood—which had plummeted at the dual realizations that not only had she not sent Baltic on his way in order to be alone with him, but she also didn't even have time to chat—rose at her change of attitude. "Oh? What is it you need help with, most lovely of all my mates?"

She ignored the reference, holding up a small box upon which two dragons had been set in silver. "I'm going to summon the First Dragon. You can help."

He watched in horror when she pulled out of the box a silk-wrapped object that turned out to be a large crystal hung on a chain. "The Avignon phylactery?" he asked, his voice almost an octave higher than usual. He cleared his throat, and said in a normal tone, "Why do you wish to speak with the First Dragon?"

"Because he can help us," she answered, gesturing to a small gray-and-white striped sofa. "Come on, we don't have much time before Anduin is up from his nap."

"Er ... Baltic—" Constantine started to protest, wildly running through objections and wondering which he could present without appearing in a bad light to Ysolde. "Why would you summon the First Dragon without Baltic?"

"Because he refuses, the stubborn boob. I've tried to get him to help me summon his dad for the last three nights, and he gets more and more annoyed, so I decided that he can be that way. I'll just do it myself. Now, sit here. You've met the First Dragon, yes?"

He stared at her, his mind dashing hither and yon like a particularly deranged squirrel.

"Oh, that's right, you were with me in the sex shop in London when he dropped in to warn me and be cryptic, per usual," she said with a distinct note of acid in her voice. "Good. That should make it easier to summon him. Come on, don't be shy. You sit next to me, and we'll both hold the phylactery, and focus on calling the First Daddy to our presence."

Constantine felt cold, deathly cold. Idly, he wondered how he could be so, since he was technically dead, but as he could think of no objection that would not show him in a cowardly light, he sat on the edge of the sofa. "I do not care in the least what Baltic thinks about my actions, but I would not have him angry at you, my sweet," he started to say, hoping to plead with her to stop without appearing to do so, but sadly, Ysolde seemed impervious to his pleas.

"Pfft," she said, dismissing the subject of Baltic's ire. "He doesn't have a leg to stand on, and he knows it. Are you ready? You take one end, and I'll take the other, and we'll focus, OK?"

Reluctantly, he pressed his thumb and forefinger to the end of the crystal that held the shard of the dragon heart, relic of the First Dragon himself, and priceless artifact of dragonkin. "Perhaps—"

Before he could say more, the air in front of them gathered itself and shimmered in an unnatural way, finally resolving itself into the figure of a man.

"Dragon sire." Constantine was instantly on his feet, bowing low, as was due the dragon progenitor.

The First Dragon's eyes were gold as they rested on the figure of Ysolde, who got to her feet more slowly. "Child of light," he said, obviously waiting for her to explain why he was there.

Constantine's palms pricked. Chivalric to the tips of his toes, he would protect Ysolde against any threat no matter how heinous the attacker or overwhelming the odds, but if she thought he was going to intervene when it came to the First Dragon, she was sadly mistaken.

"First Dragon," she said, giving him a little nod. "I realize it's been only a few weeks since we last saw you, but I thought the time was ripe to have a discussion."

The First Dragon made a show of glancing around the room, his gaze passing over Constantine without pausing.

Constantine slumped in relief, hoping against hope that perhaps the First Dragon might not have recognized him.

"And yet I do not see Baltic," the dragon sire said, his gaze continuing to hold that of Ysolde.

Constantine awarded her a full score of points for bravery. He had a feeling he would not be able to gaze back with the same equanimity as she was doing now.

"No. He forbade me to summon you." She made a dismissive motion. "You can imagine how I felt about that."

The First Dragon's lips twitched. Constantine stared at him in amazement, glancing nervously back to Ysolde.

"I can," the dragon sire said, inclining his head slightly. "It does not surprise me at all that given Baltic's stricture against doing so, I find myself here now. What is it you seek?"

"Do you know what's been going on with the red dragons?" Ysolde asked. "You do, don't you?"

Constantine thought for a moment he might swoon. He blinked a few times at Ysolde, then, with a worried glance at the First Dragon, risked invoking that august personage's attention by sidling over to his beloved former mate and whispering, "Ysolde! This is the dragon sire. The father of all dragons who ever were, and ever will be. To speak to him with such accusation is folly in the extreme."

"I know who he is," she answered, absently patting Constantine on his arm. "I also know that he professes to love all the dragonkin, and yet an entire sept has been wiped out, and we haven't heard a peep from him except a warning about a curse. I want to know why. And I want to know where the ring is that we can use against Asmodeus."

Constantine clutched the back of the nearest chair in an attempt to keep from prostrating himself before the First Dragon while pleading for mercy on Ysolde's behalf.

The First Dragon said nothing, just looked at her with his uncanny eyes.

"Dammit, you can't do this to us!" Ysolde stormed, marching forward until she was almost toe to toe with the First Dragon.

Constantine mentally started to draft a will leaving all his worldly goods to Ysolde, knowing that the point would come when he had to intervene, which might save Ysolde, but would no doubt destroy him. *Again.*

"Jian died," Ysolde continued, her eyes filling with tears, her voice throbbing with distress. "All the red dragons died. They were wiped out, or changed into horrible demonic beings. You may not care that an entire sept was wiped out, but I do!"

"I am aware of the passing of all dragonkin from one realm to another," the First Dragon said, still watching Ysolde.

"And yet you've done nothing?" she yelled, slapping her hands on her legs, her eyes blazing with fury. "How dare you? How dare you claim you care and yet do nothing when an entire sept is destroyed!"

"Ysolde!" Constantine threw caution to the wind, taking his former mate by the arm and pulling her back. He'd sworn to protect her, and he would do so, even if it spelled his own doom. "You forget to whom you speak. You cannot accost the dragon sire in this manner."

"Oh, she can. And frequently does," the First Dragon said, a martyred expression flickering across his face. "She has ever been thus, and I begin to see will ever be so."

"He can do something!" Ysolde said, struggling to get out of Constantine's grip, but he owed it to her to keep her from making what could be a tragic mistake. He hated seeing her with Baltic, but he would hate even more having her destroyed because of her passionate, if impetuous, nature. "Ask him why he hasn't done anything."

"What makes you think I have taken no action?" the First Dragon asked.

"I—you—no one said—" Ysolde, who had stopped struggling at his words, hesitated, obviously stymied by the question.

The First Dragon's gaze slid over to Constantine, who felt as if he were a bug pinned to a board. "And you, Constantine. What part do you have in protecting the weyr?"

Constantine opened and closed his mouth a couple of times before saying, "I will do whatever I can to help the dragonkin, of course, but as a spirit, I am reliant on the energy gained while I am in the spirit world and, for that reason, am not the … er … most reliable of warriors, dragon sire. I would that it was otherwise."

The First Dragon continued to watch him, making Constantine feel first very hot, then icy cold.

"You will never achieve your heart's desire if you cannot overcome that obstacle," was all the First Dragon said before looking at Ysolde again.

"I am happily mated to Baltic, which you well know, so Constantine's heart's desire is not going to happen," Ysolde said abruptly.

The First Dragon said nothing. Constantine felt as if he were encased in a block of ice. That Ysolde had misunderstood what the dragon sire was referring to was obvious, but it was equally clear that the First Dragon suffered no such confusion.

The dragon sire and he both knew what his heart's desire was, and it had nothing to do with his former mate.

"What we need from you is help ensuring that Asmodeus does not gain enough demons to destroy the rest of the septs," Ysolde told the First Dragon.

Constantine risked a glance at the demigod who had created them all. His face was impassive and unreadable as ever.

"You should help us," Ysolde continued.

The First Dragon looked thoughtful for a few seconds, finally saying, "If I did so, I would take responsibility for everything that happened to my children."

Ysolde pursed her lips, obviously wanting to say there was nothing wrong with that idea, but hesitated.

The First Dragon continued, "You would enjoy living a life where I took autonomy from you in order to keep you safe? This surprises me. I had not thought you so weak, child of light."

"I'm not weak, and of course I don't want other people making decisions for me," she answered, frowning again.

The First Dragon didn't let her continue what was sure to be a qualifier to that statement. "You have gained wisdom since I last saw you. This pleases me," he said, then with a slight smile melted into a shower of light motes that quickly faded, leaving the air in the room feeling charged with static.

"Hey! Dammit, he did it again! Argh! I just hate it when he sparkles away like that. It's so annoying," Ysolde said, and Constantine suspected she was perilously close to stomping her foot in a petulant show of temper. "He is the most aggravating, most annoying being ever!"

Constantine listened without commenting while Ysolde indeed gave in to her feelings, and ranted about how unreasonable it was that the First Dragon had so little interest in keeping bad things from happening to his own descendants.

He wanted badly to point out to her that there were few dragons—if any—who would wish to live such a life, but decided he'd leave that argument to Baltic.

For the first time since he'd met Ysolde, he had nothing but profound sympathy for Baltic, and he slipped away into the spirit world with a sense of relief that it wasn't he who would have to soothe her ire.

What did the dragon sire mean about him having to overcome the obstacle of his death to achieve his heart's desire?

He had a horrible, a very horrible idea that he would find out sooner rather than later.

My dear Friia,

I was not complaining about my kin, nor was I calling yours dull and uninspired. They are not dragons, and thus, they do not have the fiery nature that give my kin such superiority. Your descendants are not to be blamed for what they were not given. They have done very well, all things considered (Óðinn).

Your devoted brother,
First Dragon

THIRTEEN

AISLING AND THE MOTHER-IN-LAW FROM HELL. LITERALLY.

"Drake, please."

"No. Absolutely not."

"You're being ridiculous. I won't be in any danger, I swear to you."

Drake's eyes glittered with a dangerous light, but it was the dragon fire raging inside him that warned his temper was about to slip his hold. "There is nothing you can say that will alter the situation, Aisling. You are not going to Abaddon again. That you did so once without my knowledge is galling enough, but I will not have you doing so again."

I straightened up and leveled him a look that should have singed his eyebrows. "You are not the boss of me. I know you think you are, but I am a Guardian savant. It is my job to deal with demons and the denizens of Abaddon, and I will not let Jim suffer who-knows-what torments there."

"You may be a Guardian savant, but you are also my mate, the mother of my children, and carrying another child." Smoke didn't waft gently from Drake's nostrils—it damn near charged out with the same irate expression that was plastered all over the love of my life's face. "You will not put yourself at risk by attempting to rescue Jim. You don't even know for a fact that it needs rescuing."

"It's not answering my texts. It's not answering my phone calls. And the demon that Nora summoned for me said that Jim wasn't anywhere in Asmodeus's domain."

"Perhaps it has found someone to feed it, and has chosen to go with that person. Now that it is not bound to you, it may well have gone off on its own."

I just looked at him. He had the grace to look away, obviously not believing his own suggestion. "Jim is my demon. I'm responsible for it, and while it's true I don't know for certain that it's in trouble, the fact that no one has seen it or heard from it in almost a week tells me that it's being held prisoner somewhere. It's been in Abaddon for two months, Drake. I'm not going to leave it there any longer."

"You are not going to risk yourself, and that is final."

"Oh, you did not just say that!" I got to my feet when Drake turned on his heel and marched out of the sitting room just as if he had the right to tell me what I could and couldn't do. Before him, Pal and István scattered, regrouping after he passed to stare after him in surprise. Drake might not be the most even-tempered of men, but we seldom fought, and when we did, it was usually me raising my voice, not him.

I stood in the hall and yelled up at Drake as he took the stairs two at a time, "I can be just as stubborn as you can, you know. More, because I'm Irish!"

He paused at the top of the landing and looked down, an exasperated expression on his adorable face. "What the hell is that supposed to mean?"

Pal's and István's eyebrows rose. Drake seldom swore in English.

"It means I am going to Abaddon to rescue Jim, and there's nothing you can do to stop me." I spun around and stomped back into the sitting room, pulling out my phone as I did so.

A whumping sound followed me, the sort of noise a full-grown bull dragon makes leaping over the banister to the ground below, and instantly, Drake was there, spinning me around to face his fury. "You would not be so stupid."

Through the open doorway, Pal and István stood for a moment, their eyes huge, but after glancing at each other, they silently moved off to other rooms.

"Do you really think calling me names is going to make me change my mind?" I snapped, very close to losing my own temper. "You're being unreasonable."

"And you're being foolish beyond belief."

I opened my mouth to protest, but Drake suddenly pulled me into a kiss so hot it literally set the floor around us aflame. I struggled for a moment to push away from him, realized the stupidity of such an act, and kissed him back with all the love I had.

"*Kincsem*," he said a few minutes later, his voice rough with emotion. He brushed away the few errant tears that had slipped from my eyes at the thought of Jim lost and alone in Abaddon. "Do not do this."

"I have to go, Drake," I said, sniffling and pulling tissues from my pocket to dab at my nose and eyes. "I can't leave it there. I won't leave it."

"If something happened to you while you were there, I could not survive. You would risk leaving our children without parents?" he asked, smoothing his thumb across my lower lip. "And what of the babe you carry? You would not even allow him a chance to live?"

"You don't play fair," I said, more tears following the first few. "You know pregnancy hormones are running amok in me."

He pushed a strand of hair from where it got stuck on my tears. "I know you are the most valuable thing in the world to me, and I would not risk you for anything. Not even Jim."

I couldn't deny the love that shone so brightly in his eyes, and I kissed him again, embracing his fire and allowing it to fill me before sending it back to him. "I love you, too, Drake, but Jim—"

"Will not be destroyed in Abaddon. Even if it was being held prisoner—"

"No one has seen it. That means it's being held somewhere."

"—then at worst it is unhappy."

My stomach contracted at that thought. I blinked rapidly to keep back the latest rush of tears. "I can't leave it there, Drake. I'll be very careful. I'll—"

"No." He sighed a martyred sigh to end all martyred sighs. "You cannot go to Abaddon. Since I know you will not rest easy until we have the demon back, then I will simply have to go fetch it."

"You?" I gave a burble of wet laughter even as I was wiping my leaky eyes and nose again. "Sweetie, I love you to the end of time and back again, but you are not the most diplomatic of men. Smooth, yes. Urbane, you betcha. Handsome as sin, and twice as sexy? Hoo baby. But I don't think you stomping into Asmodeus's palace and demanding that Jim be handed over is going to do anything but put Abaddon at war with the dragonkin."

His brows pulled together. "We are already at war."

"All the more reason why you shouldn't go. No, if we can't go—and I still think I'd be perfectly fine going by myself, although you did manage to tug on my heartstrings with the idea of our babies left alone without us to guide them through life—then we'll just have to find someone who is more politic. Someone who wouldn't be intimidated by Asmodeus and the demons there. Someone who—"

"Where is my son? Where is my Drake, who was torn from my womb as I lay screaming on the birthing bed, my life's blood dripping from me slowly, drop by drop, while I begged the Virgin for an end to my torment? Why is he not here to greet his mama?"

I stared at Drake in growing horror. "Oh, dear gods and goddesses, please tell me that's not—"

A figure appeared in the doorway. She paused, striking a dramatic pose, all dark hair, flashing eyes, and exotic Spanish beauty. "Drake! Son of my heart!"

The martyred look that Drake had borne earlier was nothing to the one that flashed across his face before he turned to the woman preceding a whirlwind of expensive scent, even more expensive clothing, and enough dramatic gestures to choke a horse.

Doña Catalina de Elférez, mother-in-law from hell, had arrived.

"Mother," Drake said, ridding himself of the martyred expression. "You did not tell me you were intending on paying us a visit. And yet, you agreed you would do so before randomly showing up at our door."

"My love, my heart, my little boy who is thankfully nothing at all like your hell-spawn father." She kissed him on both cheeks, smiling up at him, blatantly ignoring both Drake's pointed reference to the rules regarding visits that he'd forced her to agree to, and me.

"Hello, Catalina," I said, refusing to let her run roughshod over us. I made loud air-kissing noises vaguely in her direction. "We had no idea you were coming, but I expect you planned it that way."

She sucked in her breath as she turned to look at me, her eyes narrowing. "Drakeling, what is this aged harpy who taints the air of your so pretty room? Tell it to be gone, and we shall talk about many happy things. Where are my grandchildren? They are here, yes? You must bring them down so they may greet their grand-mama."

"No," Drake said, and to Catalina's obvious surprise (not to mention mine), he spun her around and more or less marched her out into the hallway. "You know the rules, Mother. You must treat Aisling with the respect due her as my mate and mother to my children, or you may not stay here. Not that we knew you were coming, as Aisling pointed out."

"Drake! You would not treat your beloved mama in such a fashion," she started to shriek, but Catalina was no fool, and after Drake ordered Pal to gather up her luggage, she did an immediate about-face. Both physically and emotionally. "But you took my little joke as seriousness? My little one, you always were so very pedantic. Aisling, you were not so fooled, I am certain. You will tell Drake to stop being so silly and we will all get along like many little fishes in the can of oil."

"Drake, stop being silly so we can get along like sar-dines," I told the wyvern of my dreams, my lips twitch-ing despite my intentions to not give in to the case of the giggles that inexplicably were rising within me.

Drake sighed, but gestured for Pal to take upstairs the mountain of luggage with which Catalina always traveled. "Very well, but you know what I expect of your behavior. Aisling, is it not time for your rest? I'm sure the twins will be up from their nap soon, and I will take Mother to see them while you put your feet up."

"Sure," I said, happy to have an escape from what I knew was going to be a hairy visit. Catalina's always were.

"Now, my darling," Catalina said as she started up the stairs with Drake in tow. He cast me one plaintive look, but I just smiled, and shooed him onward with her. "In one of my bags, you will find sweets for my grandchildren, and in another, some toys that I picked up at a most interesting market in Rio. And for you, my darling, I have a very rare text that I found in an herbalist's shop. It is said to have been written by a mage the same year you were born, and that must be a sign, must it not? The man who had the text, he did not want to sell it to me, but you know how persuasive I can be with daggers. The man only lost one nipple, and a small amount of foreskin, really a trivial amount, before he saw the wisdom of selling it to me."

I was about to return to the sitting room in order to curl up on the couch for a little rest when Catalina's words sank into my head. "Wait!" I shrieked, my brain turning over a truly magnificent idea.

"Mate?" Drake asked, pausing midway up the stairs. "Are you having a labor pain?"

"No, it's way too early for that," I said, hurrying over to them. "But I did just birth a whopper of an idea. Catalina, how would you like to do us a favor?"

Drake first frowned; then suddenly his brow cleared as he looked at his mother with speculation in his eyes.

"A favor?" she said, looking as if she smelled something rancid.

"For Drake, not me," I said quickly, knowing well she'd never do anything if she thought it would make me happy. Hastily, I improvised a web of not-quite lies that I hoped would pique her interest. "Drake has to go to Abaddon to fetch a demon that ... er ... has information he really wants, and of course, I'm concerned because Drake is so handsome, and such a catch for any demon lord, and I just know Asmodeus will take one look at him and ... er ... fall madly in love with him."

Drake looked mildly horrified at the thought. Behind me, Pal made the choking noise of someone trying very hard not to laugh.

Catalina, however, took every compliment paid to her sons as her own, and she stopped looking like she smelled something nasty. "That is true, my Drakeling is very handsome. Both he and Kostya take after me in that regard, not their accursed father."

"And you, of course, having had experience in dealing with Magoth, are an expert in demon lords," I said, continuing to lay on the flattery with a trowel.

Luckily, Catalina liked her flattery that way.

"This is also true," she said in a thoughtful tone of voice. "I have much knowledge of the ways of such beings. Magoth—pfft. He was always telling me how evil he was, but he was weak. In the end, he did not have the stamina I require in a lover."

"Mother, we don't want you to go to Abaddon to seduce Asmodeus—" Drake started to say.

"Magoth said more than once just how masterful you were," I interrupted, giving Drake a gimlet eye while smiling widely at Catalina. I paused, and allowed doubt to cloud my expression. "Although perhaps Drake is right, and Asmodeus would be too much for you. He is, after all, the premiere prince … not a lesser one like Magoth, who was thrown out of Abaddon."

A glint of dark pleasure lit her eyes. "The first prince, you say? That is most interesting. A first prince would be agreeable, I think."

"All we would need you to do is to fetch a particular demon, not have dealings, intimate or otherwise, with Asmodeus directly," Drake said quickly.

Absently, she patted his arm and continued to look thoughtful. "Your woman says many things that are true. You know this in your heart, because you are so very much like me and feel things deeply. The premiere prince. Yes, I can see this. He would be a suitable partner. I have tired of the mortals of late, and a little trip to Abaddon to help out the son of my heart would be very welcome, I think."

Drake swore in Hungarian even as I hastily made a note of Jim's name, and its last-known location, handing the paper to Catalina. "Jim—that's the demon Drake needs you to find—is probably in the shape of a large black dog. If you could bring it out of Abaddon, and let us … er … let Drake know where to pick it up, I'm sure he'd be very grateful. Wouldn't you, sweetie?"

Drake glared at me for a few seconds, but he was never one to moan over untenable situations, and gave an abrupt nod. "We would."

"I will go as soon as I have seen my so-delightful grandchildren, and given them the presents I have brought for them, and admired how much like you they are," Catalina said, marching up the stairs without a glance down at me.

Drake followed, another martyred look on his face.

I thought of curling up on the couch in the study to rest, but a familiarity with my children had me climbing the stairs to keep an eye on how they took to their seldom-seen grandmother.

Ten minutes later I rushed down the stairs and, snatching up a magazine, sat on a chair in the entrance hall, pretending to be deeply engrossed.

"—cannot tell you how to raise your own children, who are bone of my bone, but this! Drakeling, this!"

"Mother, I warned you not to encourage Ilona to describe the birth of the kittens we gave the children. She is very literal as well as extremely precocious, and since we allowed the children to witness the birth, feeling that it would be good for them—"

"Good for them!" The words were almost a shriek as Catalina marched down the stairs, the entire front of her expensive dress now blotched and darkened by some of the rubbery goop slime that the twins loved so dearly. Tendrils of it dripped down from her dark hair, making soft little splatting noises as it hit the floor. "You call drowning me with this hell-spawn substance good for them? If I did not know that you favored me so much, I would say you were as deranged as your blighted father."

"Oh dear," I said, firmly affixing an innocent expression on my face as Catalina reached the hall. "Did something untoward, and completely and wholly amiss, happen while I was here reading this extremely captivating magazine?"

"You!" Catalina said with her usual over-the-top sense of drama, and pointed at me with one scarlet-tipped finger. "It is your influence that would so corrupt my otherwise angelic grandchildren. Drake, I shall vacate this house until such time as you may teach them some manners, and lesson your woman as to the correct way to raise them."

"Awww," I said, rearranging my expression so that now it showed nothing but dismay. "Leaving so soon?"

"Your extremely captivating magazine is upside down," Pal said as he passed by with Catalina's luggage, heading toward the front door.

"Tattletale," I said under my breath at him before turning to smile at where Drake was trying to encourage his mother to go upstairs and change her clothing.

"No," she snapped, then did another one of her lightning-fast 180-degree emotional changes, and patted his cheek. "You need me, is it not so? I would not be a mother if I could resist helping a most precious son, heart of my heart, blood of my blood, in his hour of need. I will go find the demon of whom you spoke—"

"Actually, I was the one who mentioned him, but that's beside the point," I murmured, turning the magazine the correct way up.

"—and do my duty as only a mother can know how." She sent me another scathing look that made me want to giggle, but I knew better than to do that. It would just lengthen the amount of time she ranted at Drake.

"You are hardly in a fit state to meet with anyone, let alone Asmodeus," Drake pointed out, but she brushed off his comment.

"I will go now. There is a hotel that has some very interesting equipment if you know how to persuade the manager, and I do. I will change there. Then I shall travel to Abaddon and meet with this premiere prince, and see what sort of stamina he has."

"Do you need a way into Abaddon—" I started to say, but she ignored me and was out the front door before I could get to my feet. "Should we be worried about the fact that she evidently knows entrances into Abaddon?" I asked Drake.

"It's better if we don't know," he said grimly. I had to agree.

* * *

Three days later Drake entered the playroom with his jaw tight, and his fire high. The twins, the nanny, and I were engaged in finger-painting pictures of Catalina dripping with goop, but I took one look at his expression and told the nanny to carry on without me. "What is it?" I asked when we had adjourned to the bathroom, and I was washing paint off my arms, face, and hair. "Is it Jim? Has your mom found it and brought it home?"

"Not quite." A muscle in Drake's jaw worked.

"What does 'not quite' mean in this case?" I asked, a cold feeling gripping my stomach. "She found Jim, didn't she?"

"Yes. But there was … an incident."

"Oh god. Don't tell me it tried to pee on her. It knows better than that—"

"Worse. Jim bit her." Drake took a deep breath and took my arms in both his hands. "*Kincsem*, she said the demon didn't act like a demon. It acted like a dog. It didn't speak at all, and when she addressed it by name, it didn't respond."

"Nooo!" I said on a wail, tears filling my eyes. I struggled to get free from Drake. "What have they done to poor Jim? Why did it bite Catalina? Did she hit it? Jim never bites, not even when I want it to, so I can't imagine why it would bite her unless she did something to deserve it."

"She said that Asmodeus had found it, and decided it was a spy, and ..." Drake's eyes were dark with emotion.

"What?" I asked, my lower lip trembling with the need to bawl.

"Evidently he ensured the demon would not be able to report what it found by stripping its memory."

I stared at him, simultaneously horrified and relieved. "That's ... that's terrible, but at least it didn't outright destroy Jim. Amnesia ... I have to say, that's a better situation than what Asmodeus might have done."

Drake's eyes continued to glitter with anger. "There is more, Aisling. My mother didn't say anything about how she got it free from Asmodeus, but I assume ... no. Speculation there will only lead me to madness. She messaged me that she had done as we asked, and dragged the demon to the exit to the mortal world. When she shoved it through the door, intending on hauling it to the car waiting, it turned around and bit her. That was enough for her. She let Jim loose, and returned to what I can only imagine are extremely upsetting acts of a carnal nature with Asmodeus."

"Jim is running around? Here in Paris? Without its memory? We should go look for it."

"Not Paris." Drake took another deep breath. "The exit from Abaddon that my mother used was in Poland."

"Jim's in Poland, lost?" I wrung my hands, actually wrung my hands at the thought of Jim wandering around alone, without the ability to communicate, and possibly suffering some sort of brain damage in addition to the memory loss. "What are we going to do?" I asked, feeling the hot trail of tears on my cheek.

"We will look for it. Stay here, and remain calm.

Kostya is coming by with the black dragons who are in Paris, and we will fly to Warsaw and scour the city for the demon."

I blubbered out my thanks, following Drake down to the hall. To my surprise, when Kostya entered the house, another man followed him, a very welcome sight indeed.

"Rene! Oh, thank the goddess. You're just who we need." I rushed over and gave him a hug.

He hugged me in return, and then raised a hand when I started to explain. "Did you think I would not be here the instant I heard that Jim is deranged and lost? I am here to put my taxi at your service. Or rather, a cousin's taxi in Warsaw. Naturally, I will join in the search for Jim."

"I'll go with you to look," I told him, running to grab my cell phone in case Jim came to its senses and managed to call me. "Drake and Kostya are rounding up men, as well, and if you and I search for Jim via your cousin's taxi—"

The world at that moment seemed to stop. For an instant, it was as if everything in it was frozen. I couldn't breathe, couldn't move, couldn't even so much as squawk in protest. Life just stopped ... and then suddenly it started again with an odd, unpleasant ripple in the air, like an earthquake that didn't touch the earth itself.

Drake spun around to look at me, asking, "Mate! Are you all right?"

"Yes, but that was the weirdest thing ever. What was it?"

Rene looked faintly sick. "*Mon dieu, mon dieu*! That could not be—I have heard rumors, as have we all, but it could not be—"

At that moment, Kostya lost his mind. He had staggered back a step when the ripple thing happened, and shook his head, like he was momentarily groggy. Then he looked across the hall at where Drake and I were standing, and suddenly snarled in rage.

To my horror, Drake spat out what I knew to be an extremely obscene word in Hungarian, and lunged at his brother. Kostya, always antagonistic, leaped forward at the same time, the two men going to the floor in a heap of flying fists and kicking legs.

Pal and István ran out from the back rooms, both asking what had happened, staring in surprise and horror at the scene before us.

"What the hell? Drake, stop that! Kostya, don't you dare hit him there—I said we might want more children someday! For Pete's sake—Rene, do something!"

It took a good eight minutes for us to get the two brothers separated, and even then, we had to lock Kostya into the downstairs bathroom while I mopped up blood on Drake's face. He had a split lip, a cut over his eye, and a bloody nose. "What on earth, Drake? What on the ever-loving earth?"

"I don't—I can't explain—suddenly, I felt as if Kostya was a threat to you and the children," he said around me dabbing at his hurt lip.

"I can explain," Rene said sadly, watching when Pal and István went running as Kostya yelled something from his place of confinement. "It's the curse. It has happened."

Little chills went down my arms. "Asmodeus's curse? The one against the dragons? *This* is the curse?"

Rene nodded. "Tell me, can you understand what the black wyvern is saying?" I listened for a moment, then moved into the hallway the better to hear. Drake limped after me. We both cocked our heads and focused.

"I can't," I said after a half minute of Kostya shouting. "It sounds like gibberish to me. Is he speaking Zilant?"

"No," Drake answered, frowning at the door to the bathroom. "He is not speaking any language. It is all just noises."

"It is the curse," Rene said, shaking his head. "It is as I feared. You will not be able to understand other dragons. Ones who are not in your sept."

"That's the stupidest curse in the world," I snorted, angry and worried, and wanting to shout and cry and scream at whoever was doing this to us. "Why would Asmodeus not want us to ... oh."

"Without communication, you cannot plan. You cannot consult one another. You cannot even explain what is happening." Rene shook his head again. "He is clever, that demonique one. He sets his demons against your septs, and ensures that you will not be able to band together against him."

"Divide and conquer," I said softly, almost sick to my stomach at the thought of it.

"And the antagonism?" Drake asked, touching his lip.

"It, too, is due to the curse. You are wyverns, so it hits you stronger, I think, than the others." He turned to István. "Were you compelled to attack Kostya?"

"I wanted to hit him, yes. His presence rankled," István replied. "But I did not want to kill him as Drake obviously did."

I sat down on the nearest chair, feeling all shades of despair. "Great. Now what are we going to do? Jim's lost in Warsaw without knowledge of who it is, and the dragons are cursed. Dammit, I'm a professional. I'm not going to cry..."

I cried. In the end, Rene explained to Kostya what had happened. We tried to get him out of the house with Drake making a concerted effort not to attack him, but they just jumped each other again. Pal and István got Kostya out the door, and when I went out to beg Kostya to do what he could to look for Jim, he just shook his head, and said something unintelligible before turning away and leaving.

"We will be landing shortly," Drake said a few hours later, as we circled Warsaw. He sat next to me, his gaze on the wastebasket filled with crumpled, damp tissues. "Do not cry, Aisling."

"I can't help it," I said with a soggy hiccup. "It's the pregnancy hormones. Drake, what if Jim's permanently damaged?"

"It isn't," he said firmly, pulling me tight to his side so I could absorb all the comfort he offered. "Jim is resilient, and very smart. It will survive until we can find it. Do not give up hope, mate. We will find Jim. All will be well again."

I prayed he was right. I didn't think I could face a world without my sarcastic, annoying, and utterly adorable furry little demon.

And then there was the curse to deal with. ...

I sighed. I had a feeling breaking the curse wasn't going to be easy.

My dear Friia,

I must leave the Beyond for a short time in order to keep a promise made to a wyvern. I would be happy to see you after all has been made right. Perhaps even a family reunion might be in order? It has been a very long time since I have seen all my siblings, although I suspect I might be seeing one of them sooner rather than later.

My thanks for your assistance during this trying time, and I hope you enjoy your new snorkeling instructor. I had to ask my steward what a snorkeling was, but he assures me it is a water sport that is quite pleasant.

Your devoted brother,
First Dragon

EPILOGUE

AT LAST, ALL IS MADE CLEAR. RIGHT?

From: Sally

May, darlin', you know I'm the last person in the world to interfere, but I do feel that my former other half has taken things a little too far this time. I mean, it was one thing when I was a demon lord, wasn't it? I know you would be the first person to agree that I was simply perfect for that job. What I could have done as premiere prince! Alas, that path was denied to me due to absolutely antiquated rules about the Sovereign not being allowed to head up Abaddon, as well. But that's neither here nor there, is it, really?

From: May

Um? Sally, I don't understand your text, and I'm sorry that I don't have a lot of brainpower to devote to deciphering your more-than-a-little-cryptic message, but we're having a bit of a time here what with the curse that you warned us about. The weyr has in effect been destroyed. So if you have something to say, please just say it, because Gabriel and I are busy now trying to figure out a way for the septs to break the curse without killing each other. I don't suppose you have any information about where Sasha is, do you? Gabriel thinks she might have Asmodeus's ring.

From: Sally

Beyond training as an apprentice for a variety of professions, I have no idea where Sasha is.

From: May

What about Asmodeus's ring? Do you have it?

From: Sally

Sweetness, if I had Asmodeus's ring, I could take over Abaddon, myself. The fact that I haven't says much.

From: May

Great. Just great. No one knows where this ring is, and now the dragons can't work together to locate it, and there's a curse to break, and it's all horrible.

From: Sally

As you know, I am not one for tooting my own horn, but you will notice that Asmodeus did not curse the dragonkin while I was still Sovereign. In fact, my former other half, Terrin—you remember him?—he has a demon dog now, and is parading around Scandinavia calling himself a demon lord, and joined some traveling circus to display said demon. I find that interesting, don't you? Not that I'm trying to, oh, say, send a big ole herd of dragons to the Norse lands in order to force Terrin to come to his senses—truly, can you imagine? Terrin as a demon lord? I laughed so hard at that idea that I almost snorted. Almost, because of course, no member of the Carrie Fay Academy of Perky Bosoms and Magnificent Eyebrows ever conducts herself in a manner where snorting is condoned.

From: May

Wait, what? Someone has Jim? The big black dog demon Jim? Is that what you're hinting at? If Terrin has taken Jim, then yes, we'll absolutely send a herd of dragons to teach him that he can't just steal other people's demons and pretend it's his own. Where in Scandinavia is he?

From: May

Sally? Did you get my last text? We need to know where, exactly, this former partner of yours is so we can rescue Jim.

From: May

Please, Sally. This is important!

From: Court of Divine Blood Mobile Services

We're sorry, but the number you have attempted to contact has been disconnected or disabled by the user.. For further information, please text your nearest Court representative. Have a bright and glorious day!

* * *

From: Terrin

Did you send it?

From: Sally

Sweetest of all sweet ones, did you doubt I would tattle on you the very second I could?

From: Terrin

I just hope they believe you. I found the woman you mentioned, by the way. It seems a shame to involve the whole family, but since the First Dragon was adamant, I'll contact her. The other two will have to do something pretty drastic to keep her safe, though.

From: Sally

Don't you worry there. Her family will rally around her.

From: Terrin

I have no doubt you will see to it they do.

From: Sally

Darlin', I have nothing to do with it. I'm just a simple former Sovereign enjoying some quality time in the South Pacific.

From: Terrin

...

From: Sally

All right, I may have put a word in a few ears that the demons Asmodeus sent out are looking for it, as well as the dragons, and that until things settle down a bit, it was really better the ring be tucked away somewhere safe, but it's not like I told the Charmer those things in person. That would be all sorts of wrong, now, wouldn't it?

From: Terrin

I have no doubt that the dragon progenitor will approve of the many intricate layers of your arrangements. And speaking of that, I understand about the two women, but what about the brother? Involving him won't be very nice.

From: Sally

The things we do for others. And they call me bad just because I like to be a little naughty now and again! Well, I'm off to the Azores. Enjoy your time in Sweden!

From: Terrin

You do know I'm allergic to dogs, right?

From: Terrin

Sally?

From: Terrin

sigh It's going to be a long, long summer.

* * *

From: Bee

We need to talk. I just got a text from a friend that Aoife is in trouble.

From: Rowan

What? How so?

From: Bee

She has a demon lord's ring, and everyone in the world is looking for it. For her. Including dragons.

From: Rowan

WTF? How? Why? Dear god, if they find her ... if they find out about me ... they'll crush her.

From: Bee

Exactly. She's safe for tonight—she saw some demon being destroyed, and freaked out—but they'll release her from the psych ward tomorrow if we don't do something. Rowan, the demon saw her. It will know that she has the ring, and will tell everyone else. We have to get her away. Hide her. Keep her safe where no one will be able to find her.

From: Rowan

I don't suppose it's as easy as taking the ring ... ?

From: Bee

I don't think so. I gave it to someone with whom I knew it would be safe, but you know how those sorts of magical items are—they choose the person, not vice versa. Although I really had thought it would stay with Sally ... oh well, that's a moot point now. This one has clearly chosen Aoife, and it's up to us to hide her away somewhere in order to keep her safe.

I've had an idea, but it's pretty extreme. You need to come out here, though. It's going to be rough, and it will take both of us to do it.

From: Rowan

I'll take a portal, but it will take me twelve hours to get to a city with one. Will she be safe until then?

From: Bee

I'll make sure she is. Just don't delay. And don't let any of the dragons hanging around see you!

From: Rowan

Christ. That's all we need. Be there as soon as I can.

From: Bee

I just hope that someday, she forgives us ...

A NOTE FROM KATIE

My lovely one! I hope you enjoyed reading this book, which I handcrafted from the finest artisanal words just for you. If you are one of the folks who likes to review books, I'd love it if you posted a review for it on your favorite book spot. If you aren't a reviewing type, fear not, I will cherish you regardless.

I'd also like to encourage you to sign up for the exclusive readers' group newsletter wherein I share behind-the-scenes info about my books (and dogs, and love of dishy guys, and pretty much anything else that I think people would enjoy), sneak peeks of upcoming books, news of readers'-group-only contests, etc. You can join the fun by clicking on the SUBSCRIBE TO KATIE'S NEWSLETTER link on my website at

www.katiemacalister.com

ABOUT THE AUTHOR

For as long as she can remember, Katie MacAlister has loved reading. Growing up in a family where a weekly visit to the library was a given, Katie spent much of her time with her nose buried in a book.

Two years after she started writing novels, Katie sold her first romance, *Noble Intention*s. More than sixty books later, her novels have been translated into numerous languages, been recorded as audiobooks, received several awards, and have been regulars on the *New York Times, USA Today*, and *Publishers Weekly* bestseller lists. Katie lives in the Pacific Northwest with two dogs, and can often be found lurking around online.

You are welcome to join Katie's official discussion group on Facebook, as well as connect with her via Twitter, Goodreads, and Instagram. For more information, visit her website at www.katiemacalister.com